Ashes to Ashes

The Pyre of Karma

By

Haimes Hensley

ISBN: 978-0-692-16371-9

ACKNOWLEDGMENTS

To our family and friends, we love you and thank you for your encouragement and patience while we created Ashes to Ashes, The Pyre of Karma.

To Stuart Rothenberg, your brilliance and creativity will 'shine on.'

To Allen, 'Doc,' best friend, confidant, and love, thank you from the heart.

For Mom. We miss you.

BOOKS
The Hand Of Karma
Ashes to Ashes, The Pyre of Karma

CHAPTER ONE

Jane wrapped herself in an old multi-colored afghan to fend off the cold and curled up on the musty beat-up sofa. They were almost out of propane and she didn't know when Thurman would bring enough money home to order more. The heater banged hard when it kicked on. She hoped keeping the thermostat set at sixty degrees would get them through the bitter cold night. *One day at a time, Jane. One day at a time.*

It was now past noon and the sun had not broken through the clouds long enough to warm the dilapidated excuse for a home.

She went to the window, leaned against the frame, and pulled the afghan tight around her. Stark barren trees stood like frozen soldiers who waited for their orders to advance. Far back into the woods the green of the pines gave the only color to the day. The sky was a dismal gray. It seemed like winter would never end.

Jane cradled her growing belly with her hands and felt the baby flutter. She hummed a quiet melody to her precious child, certain she carried a girl. The baby's father, Thurman, insisted she couldn't possibly know. Undeterred, she had secretly chosen the perfect name, Scarlett. For a few precious seconds, tender thoughts of the new life inside of her helped her escape from her miserable existence.

She covered her protruding belly with the afghan as if to shield her child from some unseen danger. Jane wondered if her mother ever felt this kind of love for her. Jane had been a ward of the state since she was an infant. She was six years old when she asked her foster-mother about her real family and was told they knew very little about her birth parents. Her father was unknown. Her mother was a fifteen-year-old Native American runaway who died of a drug overdose. The first real love Jane ever felt was from her foster-sister, Ann. However, when Ann turned eighteen and moved out of the home, they lost touch.

If only she could see her again.

Jane was about to step away from the chill that seeped through the cracked window when movement down the lane caught her attention. It was the same green car that drove by this morning. It slowed almost to a stop. The mobile home they lived in was so isolated deep in the woods that it was odd to see any vehicle other than Thurman's red truck this far back from the paved road. Maybe they were hunters.

Another loud shutter from the heater warned her that Thurman had to get propane before she and the baby froze to death.

It had been weeks since she was plagued by horrific morning nausea. Now she was hungry all the time. With the crocheted blanket draped over her shoulders, she walked into the kitchen, her socked feet cold on the worn linoleum, emptied the last of the stale cereal into a bowl and poured some of the watered-down powdered milk into it. No matter how many times Thurman told her she'd get used to the taste of powdered milk, she never would. She went back to the sofa, spread out the blanket, drew her ice-cold feet up under the cover, and began to eat her breakfast. Her eyes brimmed with tears. *How did everything get so screwed up?*

She had to pee so often these days. She was forced to leave the warmth of the blanket and hurried to the bathroom. The small frosted window let in scant light. She lit the candle kept on the back of the commode, the broken light fixture dangled overhead by a single wire. Another project Thurman promised to take care of but never did. The dump of a home they lived in belonged to Thurman's buddy Fred who told them they could live there rent free if Thurman would fix it up. *If only he would.*

2

She and Thurman met when she was a painfully shy seventeen-year-old. He was her first boyfriend, had been sweet and considerate, and wanted to marry her when she told him she was pregnant, just before her eighteenth birthday. That same week she moved out of the foster home and into the trailer with Thurman. Jane brought with her one suitcase filled with clothes, and one grocery bag which contained cherished memorabilia from some of the happy times she had growing up with Ann . . . the picture of them dressed alike in their blue dotted Swiss dresses, her Chatty Cathy doll missing most of its hair, and their favorite book, *Gone With The Wind* that Ann would read to her at bedtime.

She blew out the candle and returned to the living room where she laid down on the sofa, snuggled under the cover, and dozed off.

"Hey, where's my supper?" Jane woke at the sound of his slurred words. "You gonna lay there when your man comes home? Why's it so cold in here—I'm 'bout to freeze m'balls off." His drunken stench filled the room.

"Did you bring groceries, we're out of everything." He didn't answer. "And it's cold in here Thurman because we're almost out of propane. I'm trying to make it last. You said you'd order it today when you went to town. Did you?"

He gave her that look that made chills run up her spine. "Ran outta money," his words muddled. "How's I suppose to buy propane?"

She knew better than to press him right now and lowered her eyes to diffuse his temper.

The next morning started out as every morning had for the last couple of months; filled with sadness, despair, and hunger. She didn't care about the hunger as much for herself as she did for the baby. Out of habit, she went to the kitchen and opened the refrigerator. It didn't take more than a glance to see that the food fairies hadn't come while they slept. The shelves were bare. She wasn't about to waste what little propane might be left to heat up the water tank and opted to turn on the cold water spigot to get washed.

A wave of desolation and depression hit her. Without a telephone, she was even more disconnected from the world than the remoteness of where she lived made her feel. She clung to the promises Thurman had made to her. Things would get better soon but, how could they? The money he made from working odd jobs around town he mostly spent on whiskey and cigarettes.

Alerted by the sound of tires on the gravel driveway, she wiped tears from her face and went to greet Thurman who entered the kitchen with two arm loads of groceries. He put the brown paper bags on the Formica table and flung two crumpled twenties on the counter.

"Now you can fix me something to eat and while you're at it, turn the damn heat up. It's freezin' in here." He watched her walk to the thermostat in the living room. "Baby, you still got the best ass in Ohio. I'm hard just lookin' at you."

"Well, this ass is freezing, Thurman. We need to get the tank filled before it runs out."

"Ordered it today, babe. It'll be here before supper." He walked up behind her and wrapped his arms around her belly. He whispered, "If money keeps comin' in like this, we'll get married soon."

She wanted to ask him where the money came from but thought better of it.

"Jane, you know I'm sorry about drinking too much yesterday, right?"

"Sure." She kissed him on the cheek. "By the way, Thurman, I need to go to the clinic soon. Can you drive me over next week? I'm pretty far along now and haven't seen a doctor yet. You know how important—"

"Damn it all to hell, Jane. There you go again, complaining. Didn't I bring groceries home? Didn't I bring home money? Didn't I order propane? Baby, why you always gotta bring up the one damn thing I didn't do?" He stomped to the kitchen cabinet, took down the bottle of whiskey and poured it into a stained mug.

She hated it when he drank—he got mean. Thurman's pushes and shoves had gotten harder and he had started something new. Whenever she 'made him get real mad' he would take one of her few possessions and destroy it. Last week he tore pages out of her precious copy of *Gone With The Wind*, threw them into the trash barrel and set them on fire. He yelled, "This is what you deserve slut!" The smoke from the pyre drifted away like her fantasy to give her little girl a good life.

Maybe Thurman was right. This life is what she deserved for getting pregnant before she got married but he knew he was the first and only man she had ever dated.

#

Over the last few weeks, Jane walked as if she was on eggshells, afraid of setting Thurman off again. She didn't know what she had done this time to trigger his rage. A cold cloth pressed to her bruised and swollen face, Jane went to the kitchen, slid the faded curtain aside and gazed out of the window. Tree branches were covered with ice from a late winter storm. Jane turned from the window dreading Thurman's return home contrite with his usual apology, "Baby, I swear I'll never hit you again."

She had endured his physical abuse and drunken temper and had forgiven him one too many times. The last straw came yesterday when in a fit of rage, Thurman dragged her outside in her bare feet and forced her to watch him burn the picture of Ann and her in their dotted Swiss dresses. The loss of her precious treasure hurt more than his fist.

She rubbed her heavy belly and felt so much love for the life growing inside of her. "You won't grow up in this hell, my sweet little angel."

Jane lay awake too nervous to sleep. By dawn she had reviewed her plan over and over until she was certain she had thought of every possibility. Thurman's alarm clock buzzed. She lay still and felt the mattress shake when he got up to go to his temporary job at the lumber yard. Her breath was shallow as she listened to every move he made . . . into the bathroom, into the kitchen, back to the bedroom, return to the living room. The front door closed. He started the truck and left. She remained motionless and prayed he would stick to his schedule.

She listened for any sign of Thurman's return. Jane sat up and moved to the side of the bed. After what seemed an eternity, she stepped onto the cold floor and began what she had rehearsed in her mind. Get dressed. Check the driveway. Grab suitcase . . .

She tossed the beat-up suitcase on the bed. It would hold the sum total of her eighteen years on earth: her clothes from the dresser and the ripped up remains of her book. She grabbed the afghan off the sofa and shoved it into the battered suitcase.

Another check of the driveway—no sign of Thurman. Jane bent under the bed and reached for the mug she kept hidden near the back of the headboard. She managed to collect a few dollars in change she found in Thurman's work pant pockets from time to time; $12.63. It wouldn't go far, but that would have to do.

On her way out, she spotted the jar of peanut butter on the kitchen counter, shoved it into her coat pocket, and put on her knitted hat. She took one last look around, "Say goodbye to this life, Scarlett. Mama's gonna take good care of you from now on." The baby kicked a reassuring thump and Jane was out the door and on her way to a better life.

Jane stayed close to the tree line and crept along the side of the driveway prepared to hide at the first glimpse of Thurman's truck. Her heart pounded. She reached the dirt lane—one step closer to freedom. The lane would lead her to the main road and then to town where she'd catch the first bus to her foster parents' home in St. Paris. She was sure they would help her. It was twenty miles away but to her it was another world.

The bitter cold wind whipped around her. Jane stepped off the road and removed the afghan from the suitcase. She wrapped it around her and continued on her way, careful to avoid patches of ice. A loud *crack* and Jane bolted to the bushes then discovered it was an ice-laden branch that had broken. If she wasn't so scared she would have laughed at herself.

The sound of an engine. She stopped. Tires on frozen earth. Louder. Closer. She scrambled and hid behind the bramble of last year's blackberry patch and held her breath. The vehicle drove right past her. She exhaled. It wasn't Thurman's truck, but the green car she had seen drive by their place. Relieved, she climbed out from behind the bushes and picked up her pace.

She hadn't gone far when the rumble of a vehicle came from behind. She dashed off the road and stumbled into a small gully. The green car drove by. Jane stood and rubbed her cold scrapped hands and stepped out onto the road. Seconds later, the green car came to an abrupt halt ahead of her, backup lights came on, and the car skidded to a halt a few feet in front of Jane.

"Where the hell you think you're goin', girl?" Thurman bellowed, "Get in and bring your shit with you."

Filled with terror, Jane wet her pants. "Whose . . . car . . . is . . . this?" she stammered.

"It's Fred's. I use it to see what you're up to when I'm not home. Lucky for me I drove by today. Throw that crap in the back and get in."

Jane lowered her head and climbed onto the front seat. He stomped on the gas pedal so fast that the passenger door slammed shut and hit her shoulder. He made a quick U-turn on the dirt road and drove onto the gravel driveway. He sped up to the trailer, threw the gear into park, reached across the seat and dragged her out of the car from the driver's side. Her belly banged into the steering wheel.

"Thurman, please don't . . ."

He backhanded her across the face. Her nose poured blood. "You'll never leave me! Do you understand?" he screamed, his voice falsetto with rage. With a vice-like grip on her arm, he dragged her up to the front porch. Jane stumbled against the wooden steps. Skin peeled off her shins.

Thurman opened the front door and shoved Jane inside. She fell to her knees. "Thurman, I love you. Please don't do this!"

He yanked her by the hair and flung her onto the sofa. "You'll never leave me. Never! DO YOU HEAR ME?"

#

For a week, Jane was chained to cinder blocks in the second bedroom. She could move around the room far enough to reach the bucket in the corner that he left for her to use as a toilet.

With meals of only powdered milk, cereal, and canned pork 'n beans, her waif-like body was too weak to resist his repeated rapes and sodomy.

Thoughts of escape were outweighed by the terror of re-capture.

She woke to the sound of truck tires on gravel. Thurman left before she had a chance to plead with him to loosen the chain around her swollen ankle. The intermittent backache she had for the last couple of days had intensified. By mid-morning, she was hit with a powerful contraction.

Alone and terrified and in excruciating pain, she cried out, "No God, it's too soon!" She sobbed and endured hours of hard labor. The mattress on the floor upon which she lay was soaked with blood. Something was terribly wrong, but Jane was helpless.

She heard the truck return and the thud of Thurman's heavy work boots on the front steps.

She felt a gush of fluid between her legs and she screamed.

The bedroom door burst opened, "What the hell?"

"Help me, Thurman," she pleaded. With another scream, Jane bore down and felt the infant slide out. "Thurman," she begged with a weak voice, "give me my baby."

He turned and left the room.

Jane reached down onto the wet and bloody mattress and lifted the tiny blue and lifeless infant. She drew her baby to her chest. "Oh God, oh God!" She swiped her finger into Scarlett's mouth to clear the mucous and thumped her back. Nothing. She blew her breath into the baby's mouth. Nothing. "Please Thurman, help me!" she screamed. Again, and again she blew into Scarlett's mouth. Nothing.

Thurman entered the room and tossed a threadbare bath towel to Jane. "You may as well quit. It ain't alive."

With a pain in her heart beyond description, Jane tenderly wrapped the towel around the cold limp body of her little girl, clutched the dead infant to her chest, and sobbed until she fell asleep from exhaustion, Scarlett still in her arms.

The stench of his sweaty body mixed with the smell of liquor woke Jane. She was in his bed, chained and naked except for a towel between her legs. She rubbed her flaccid belly. "Thurman, where . . ."

"I buried it out back."

She rolled away from him and stared at the chain tightly wrapped around her ankle and padlocked, the other end of the chain woven through cinder blocks on the floor next to the bed.

"You hear me?" He poked her in the back. "What else could I do? It was dead."

Jane remained silent.

Thurman removed the shoelace from around his neck from which a key dangled and unlocked her restraint. "Go clean yourself up. You stink like a gutted deer."

She focused her gaze on the key.

He replaced the shoelace around his neck and left the room.

#

Over the weeks that followed, Thurman worked sporadically which meant he'd chain her to the cinder blocks. As long as he was home, he allowed her to walk around the rooms unencumbered. Jane moved about as if in a stupor. She didn't know how much longer she could get away with her zombie-like act, but for the most part, he didn't make any demands on her.

Her infected ankle healed, and her strength began to return. As the weeks passed, Thurman allowed her more freedoms during the day, but when they went to bed, he tied her wrist to his.

Half asleep, squinting against the morning sunlight that streamed through the un-curtained bedroom window, Jane felt a presence in the room and opened her eyes. Thurman loomed over her.

"It's about time you got up. I just brought groceries home."

For the first time since her escape attempt, he had left her alone and unrestrained.

"Baby, I've been thinking. You've been such a good girl. I'm willing to give you another chance. Let's start over, like we were when we first met. You were so sweet and undemanding. Remember how you laughed at my jokes? If you could do that, maybe we could get married." He finished his soliloquy, told her to get cleaned up and start breakfast.

Stunned speechless, she thought he had totally lost his mind. Start over? Marry him?

Thurman studied Jane as she made breakfast while he sat at the rickety kitchen table. "See how nice it can be Jane when it's just the two of us?" Strips of bacon sizzled in the cast iron skillet. "That sure smells good. Remember baby, I like it crisp . . . and make sure to save that grease for gravy and biscuits tomorrow."

Jane poured the rendered fat into an empty Maxwell House can then took the plate of crisp bacon and placed it in front of Thurman who had scooted himself up to the table.

"I want to put a cross on Scarlett's grave, Thurman."

He shoved a strip of bacon into his mouth and said, "You gave it a name?"

"She wasn't an 'it' Thurman. She was our baby."

"There is no 'Scarlett's' grave. I burned the damned thing in the trash drum," he said, chomping on another piece of bacon. "Now don't bring this shit up again. Hurry up with those eggs." He turned back to his plate.

Behind him, her hand flew to her mouth. Her scream was silent. She returned to the gas stove, grabbed the handle of the cast iron skillet with both hands, walked over to Thurman, and with all of her might she swung.

He went down onto the linoleum. Blood trickled from his ear.

Jane put the cast iron skillet back on the burner and turned it up high. She put the remaining bacon in the pan then dipped the dishtowel into the coffee can until it was soaked with bacon fat. What grease remained in the can, she threw on Thurman, lit the towel and flung it across the room. It landed on his head and burst into flames.

The kitchen started to fill with smoke. Jane ran to retrieve her mud-caked coat and the still-packed suitcase from the closet where Thurman threw them the day he captured her. By the front door, she spotted the truck keys and his wallet on the arm of the sofa. She took what money was in the wallet and thought about taking the truck but decided to leave behind all that represented her life with Thurman.

By now the kitchen was fully engulfed.

She stepped outside and into the sunshine of a beautiful spring morning. She closed the front door behind her. "Ashes to ashes."

CHAPTER TWO

Tampa, Florida – Present Day

The unmarked police-issued squad car sat with the windows closed for several hours at the crime scene. The stink of stale cigarette smoke hit Detective Michael Vega in the face as he opened the door to the vehicle. It had been over a month since he had his last cigarette, but the interior of his car still reeked of nicotine. As unpleasant as the acrid smell of lingering smoke was, it wasn't enough to camouflage the stench of the victim's body fluid that clung to Michael's clothes. The bloated corpse had been discovered near the nature trail by a jogger. Michael was the first cop on the scene in the woods early this morning and nearly stepped on the dead man hidden in the high grass.

Michael would stop home to change before he went back to the station.

On the drive to his house, the car windows were down and the air conditioner on full blast aimed right at his face. It did nothing to alleviate the putrid odor of decomposition that surrounded him from the three-day-old cadaver.

Concerned to see the garage door of his house open and his wife's car inside when she wasn't due home from work for hours, he touched the hood. From the coolness of the metal, he could tell Teresa's car must have been there for a while. He thought she might have one of her migraines again. She'd been coming home more often with headaches.

Michael closed the garage door, kicked off his shoes, stripped down to his boxers and shoved his clothes into the washing machine. The hot water cycle started as he opened the interior garage door and stepped into the house.

"Teresa . . . you here?" he called out as he made his way through the family room. The new 70" flat screen television she gave him for their twentieth anniversary last week, hung over the fireplace. He was bowled over that day when he came home from work to find she had it installed and then handed him the gift-wrapped remote control.

Their mid-century home was in an established neighborhood. The house was perfect for the two of them. They had built a good life together and he looked forward to the Mediterranean cruise next month that he had given her for twenty happy years of marriage.

Her jacket and purse were draped on the dining room chair. Michael noticed she had drawn the drapes in the living room and the house was quiet. For as long as he'd known her, Teresa had suffered with chronic migraines and would have to lay down in a darkened room until it passed. Michael remembered their first date and how disappointed Teresa was at their high school prom when she developed a debilitating headache, got sick to her stomach, and they had to leave before their first dance.

The master bedroom was on the opposite side of the house. Michael headed to the closed door. Careful not to disturb her in case she was asleep, he turned the knob with ease and pushed open the door to the darkened room.

His eyes saw but his mind needed to process. He felt like he was suspended in time. His wife, his Teresa, was having sex with another man. "What the hell, Teresa?"

"Oh, my God!" Teresa screamed and yanked the sheet up over her naked body. "Michael. . . let me explain." Teresa yanked the sheet off the bed and wrapped it around her which left her shocked lover totally exposed. She sprang from the bed and ran toward Michael.

Blinded by rage, Michael shoved her aside, lunged at the naked man and screamed, "You son-of-a-bitch! I'll kill you!" He grabbed Bill Lang, his captain, by the arm and dragged him off the bed. Michael walloped him in the face with a right cross hard enough to send him crashing into the wall. He grabbed the stunned naked man by the hair and continued to pummel. With each punch to the face, blood sprayed from the bastard's mouth. Lang slumped to the floor splayed on his back.

A broken front tooth had cut into Michael's fist.

At the precise second Michael drew his foot back and took aim at the man's limp dick, the guy pulled his legs up to protect himself. The heel of Michael's foot connected with the side of Lang's knee.

"Jesus Christ, Vega! You broke my leg!"

In a burst of fury, Michael grabbed the brass lamp off the dresser, raised it over his head and—

"Stop!" Teresa screamed. "You're going to kill him!"

Sickened by the sight of Teresa going to the aid of her lover, Michael scooped Lang's clothes from the chair and flung them into the hallway. "Both of you, get out!" Michael shoved a limping Lang out of the room. Teresa trailed behind.

Slumped on the edge of the bed, his head in his hands, Michael cried.

#

Michael felt the eyes of his fellow officers watch him with pity as he cleared his belongings from his desk. The heartache he experienced from his wife's betrayal was equal to the humiliation he felt when he discovered how many people in the department knew about the affair Teresa was having with his superior.

Captain Lang had as much to lose as Michael if Internal Affairs pursued the incident. Lang claimed his injuries happened when he slipped off a ladder. Michael said a dog bit him on the hand. He knew nobody bought their stories but the only way he could avoid scrutiny by I.A. was to take an early retirement and get out with his pension. An investigation would have resulted in Lang being demoted, however his career would have been protected by his rank and his connections within the department. Michael might have been seen as the aggressor and could have been fired and lost his pension. He wouldn't take that chance. Regardless, Michael knew his career with the Tampa Police Department was over.

Nineteen years in and he was brought down by a backstabbing brother in blue.

His early retirement accepted, and papers signed, Michael made his way past co-workers who patted him on the back, shook his hand, and wished him well. A few winked 'thanks for decking the prick.' Michael had no regrets for beating the shit out of Lang but for what he lost, his marriage and his career, he should have put him in the morgue.

Michael walked through the Tampa P.D. building for the last time, as a cop. A rookie, accompanied by a Field Training Officer, held open the heavy glass door of the building as Michael exited. He mumbled a 'thanks' and didn't wait for conversation.

A group of off-duty guys who lingered outside gave Michael a nod as he walked by.

He felt his cellphone vibrate on his belt. It was Teresa again. "Shit." He ignored the call. Michael suspected she was about to leave another desperate message begging for forgiveness. The frequency of her calls bordered on harassment. Her suggestion to use the cruise to save their marriage was ludicrous and pitiful. How could she not accept that what she did was unforgiveable?

"Hey buddy. You got the time?"

Michael spotted his old friend Steve DeMarcou leaning against the car. Friends since they went through the police academy, in some ways, Michael felt as close to Steve as he did his own kid brother, George. They had shared a lot over the years, struggling through the academy, week-long fishing trips, the softball league, family gatherings . . .

Michael swallowed hard, "Hey man, what are you doing here?"

"Where else would I be?" Steve put his hand on his friend's shoulder. "Come on, let's get out of here."

CHAPTER THREE

The small apartment Michael leased since his separation from Teresa was on the opposite side of town. He wanted a fresh start far away from his wife, the department, and the betrayal that he couldn't forgive.

The rental complex had amenities that most people would enjoy; a pool, a gym, a tennis court, but he had no interest in them or in the people who lived in the complex. He wanted solitude.

Michael carried a bag of groceries from his car, approached the building and almost tripped over a soccer ball that bounced in front of him.

"Sorry, mister," a freckled-faced kid called out.

"No worries," Michael tapped the ball back to the boy and was reminded of how he and his brother George played soccer when they were kids. He remembered how George hand-painted an Easter Egg to resemble a soccer ball and hid it in Michael's basket. When he cracked it open, the egg was raw and splattered on Michael's new Easter suit. George rolled on the floor laughing, "The yolk is on you!" Michael missed his kid brother and his bizarre sense of humor.

Michael entered his apartment, put the bag of groceries on the kitchen counter and unloaded the frozen dinners, peanut butter and jelly, bread, and milk. That was the extent of the cooking he would do for himself. He eyeballed the living room, devoid of furnishings except for the unpacked boxes that lined the wall, a kitchen chair and tv tray. They contained everything he took when he walked away from his marriage. A trash can filled with crumpled fast food bags was in the kitchen; a box spring and mattress on the floor in the bedroom. It was a poor excuse for his home, however temporary it might be.

Lost in limbo, it was another restless night for Michael in pursuit of sleep instead of bad guys. He awoke with his usual miserable backache, stretched, and groaned.

There was a loud knock at the front door, the kind cops used to signal their authority. A hurried mail carrier delivered a certified letter from Michael's attorney. He signed the receipt and closed the door. Inside the stark room, he sat on the lone chair and laid the envelope on the tv tray next to him. Michael had anticipated this day but didn't expect the reluctance he felt about reading what he knew was the final divorce decree. He brooded for a while then forced himself to read the documents and shoved them back inside the envelope.

His wife, parents, and brother were the solid foundation upon which he had built his life. *What a crock of shit.* How could he have been so clueless, so trusting, so damn blind when it came to Teresa? The guys at work said his mind was like a human calculator; that he could read a perp or a vic like a book. They joked that he must have ESP, something he vehemently denied. They called him a natural born lie detector.

From childhood his mother Rosaria, whose Latin heritage supported her endless superstitions, insisted that because of his premature birth and how hard he fought to survive that the angels blessed him with 'second sight.' He disagreed with her claim, but he would admit to having an analytical mind. Events in his life were dealt with logic; black and white. There was no room in his world for gray.

How could he have missed the signs of Teresa's infidelity?

Most of his adult life had been enviable. He was respected by the people he worked with, had a nice home, had a loving relationship with his wife, and was a faithful husband no matter how many temptations came his way. He'd lost track of the number of times he was propositioned by some bimbo trying to get out of trouble or by a female deputy who let him know that 'she wouldn't say no' to an off-duty tryst.

Michael was a rookie the first time he told his father that a woman tried to negotiate getting out of a DUI arrest by exposing her breasts and offering a blow job. He could still hear his father's robust laughter as he told Michael it wouldn't be the last time that would happen. His father became serious and said, "You were brought up to be an honorable man. Remember that. It's a privilege to wear that badge." How he missed those father/son, cop to cop, conversations.

The sound of Michael's cellphone on the counter brought him back to present.

"Vega."

"Michael. It's Connor Johns. How the hell are you?"

"Connor? I haven't heard from you since you moved to Philly." Michael thought it odd that his father's law enforcement partner and best friend called at the precise moment he was reminiscing about his dad. "The question is Connor, how the hell are YOU?" Michael had no desire to rehash everything that had happened to him since the last time they saw each other, not now.

"A lot better than you, I suspect. I talked to Lucarella at Tampa P.D. today. It's a damn shame what happened." Connor hesitated. "I always liked Teresa. She was so good to us when Betty was sick and so helpful after Betty died. I never would have suspected Teresa would do something like that. Your father would be heartbroken. I'd like to get my hands on Bill Lang, that bastard. How are you holding up, kid?"

Since the death of Michael's father, Connor had an uncanny way of showing up whenever Michael needed him, even if Michael was unaware of the need.

Connor and his wife Betty were there to support his mother and the family. They also tried to help fill the void in Michael and George's life, left by their father's death. Though after Betty's cancer diagnosis, all of Connor's time and attention was directed to her care.

"Connor, I appreciate your concern but . . . it's done and over with. I really don't want to talk about it."

"Well, Michael, I hope you're not blaming yourself for what Teresa did."

"No, Connor." Michael looked at the pile of boxes on the floor. "I'm really okay. How's retirement treating you?"

Connor laughed. "I couldn't take the boredom. Got my P.I. license and bought a business here in Philly, Society Hill Investigations, Inc.," he said with pride.

Michael heard him puff on what he suspected was Connor's trademark cigar. "You still smoking after your heart attack?"

"No, the doc told me I had to quit so I got one of these vapor cigarettes. At least I can pretend I'm smoking." Connor was interrupted by someone in his office and excused himself. When he returned, he said, "Michael, I'll call you later. I have to get a video tape over to an insurance adjuster before they settle a case. We caught his guy on video, climbing a ladder to trim a tree. The knucklehead's trying to get six figures from Worker's Comp. Claims he needs a wheelchair to get around. You know the old saying, 'God must love stupid 'cause he made so much of it.'"

"Ain't that the truth!" Michael laughed for the first time in a long time. He felt better after the call and realized that Connor was right. He had gone through enough. It was time to get his head out of his ass.

He picked up his keys and headed to a furniture store.

CHAPTER FOUR

It was an easy progression for Michael and Connor to renew their bond. Calls became more frequent. Connor's regular prodding and encouragement convinced Michael not only to get his P.I.'s license but to start his own company. Connor said it would be a benefit to both his morale and his finances.

The spark of enthusiasm that Connor incited within Michael started him on the fast track to acquire his Florida credentials. In the short time since he started Vega Investigations, he had more work than he anticipated. He no longer had time to dwell in the past and focused solely on his future. The majority of cases that Michael received came from lawyers he knew through the department. The jobs were straightforward and lucrative, though in comparison to police work, they bordered on the mundane.

The seasonal influx of snowbirds to Florida in the Fall increased the number of accident insurance cases.

Connor was right. This work made Michael feel like his old self again. He was now in control, productive, and his bank account didn't suck.

Blue-black storm clouds rolled in from the west. Frequent thunder and bolts of lightning warned of the pending deluge. Michael respected the dangerousness and intensity of Florida lightning storms. His camera was balanced on the dashboard and aimed at the subject. The wall of rain approached, and he tried to calculate how much time he had before the downpour and before the subject, who was suspected of insurance fraud, abandoned his project of unloading thirty bags of mulch from a pick-up truck in his driveway. Michael filmed the man loading the large bags into the truck at a garden center, tailed him home, and recorded him carrying them to his backyard. The subject claimed the pain and numbness in his legs that he experienced from an auto accident made it impossible to walk unaided and that he was 'practically a prisoner in his own home.'

The insurance company's attorney would find this video very helpful.

#

The predicted Category 2 hurricane that was due to hit Titusville, Florida veered north up the east coast of the state and was headed for North Carolina. It hit the Outer Banks as a Category 1, nonetheless the storm affected the weather in Tampa. It was hot and humid, not typical for late Fall. Sweat rolled down Michael's face as he stood behind a tree, his camera at the ready. The overwhelming humidity distracted him long enough to blot his cheek with his shirt sleeve. He returned his attention to the subject he had under observation in time to see the woman remove her knee brace and join a group of people in a game of Frisbee.

Snap. Snap. Snap.

"Gotcha!"

He walked the dirt path back toward his car when he got a call. Eager to get the a/c turned on, he waited until he started the engine before he answered.

Connor got right to the point. "Michael, I need a favor. Do you have time to do a job for me in Orlando? My guy assigned to the case just had a heart attack and is laid up for a while. I'd need you to start right away. It shouldn't take more than a week since the subject is due to return to Philadelphia next Friday."

"I might have to rearrange a couple of things, but, sure," Michael replied. "What are the details?"

"I've got a client who insists his wife is cheating. He's got a straightforward pre-nup. She screws around, she gets nothing. I've been working this case here in Philly for a couple of weeks and haven't found any dirt on her. The husband says she's taking a girls' vacation with her sorority sisters at the Ritz-Carlton. He doesn't buy it for a minute. He thinks she's screwing the contractor who worked at their house and is meeting him in Orlando."

"What's your feel, Connor?"

"It doesn't matter. I'm paid to deliver the facts. All I know is the husband won't let it go. I'll email you the particulars of the case."

The subject's description, photo, and hotel information were included in the report that Connor emailed to Michael's office. The thirty-five-year-old blonde, Jackie Pennington, was two decades younger than her husband. Married five years. No children. Husband has political aspirations.

Michael packed the equipment he would need for the job. He checked the new high resolution digital camera with audio that was designed to look like a slim profile cellphone. It was his most recent purchase of spyware equipment complete with a pin point lens on the top edge of the case. That feature made it convenient for recording while it was positioned flat on any surface and would be innocuous.

He phoned his brother George, a freelance photographer who worked from home and made himself available whenever Michael asked for his help. George was a good wingman and proved himself valuable on a number of Michael's recent jobs. George loved 'playing spy,' as he called it.

The next afternoon, Michael and George left for Orlando. It was an easy hour and a half drive to central Florida from Tampa. The brothers arrived at the luxury hotel by four p.m. and opted to park in the lot to gain an inconspicuous vantage point of the hotel entrance and of the guests.

George stayed in the car and reviewed the file and photographs of Jackie Pennington while Michael went inside to register for his room. He returned to his vehicle and saw that George had slumped down on the passenger seat and turned his shirt collar up like

Humphrey Bogart. Michael shook his head, then joined his brother.

"Any sign of her?" he asked George who held the 8x10 color print of the subject.

"Not yet," George said. He looked again at the picture. "Man, she's gorgeous. No mystery why her husband wants to keep an eye on her." George sat up and looked out of the window. "Hey, wait a minute." He pointed to a car that was approaching the valet.

There she was, Jackie Pennington and three other women. She was the only blonde in a group of brunettes. All of them were knockouts—tall, slender, and looked like they spent a lot of time at the gym. They chatted while the doorman loaded their designer luggage onto a cart and walked into the hotel.

The brothers gave them a slight lead before they pursued. If the subject suspected she was being shadowed, Michael could get burned. The two men continued past the front desk where the women waited to register. Michael and George entered the lounge adjacent to the lobby and sat at the bar where they had an unobstructed view of the four ladies as they entered the elevator.

George got up and walked to the Bell Captain's desk. On the pretext of looking up information, he fidgeted with his phone while he strained to overhear the bellman receive his instructions to deliver the women's luggage to the fifth floor.

The uniformed bell captain turned to George, "May I help you, sir?"

"Yes, thank you. This is my first time in Orlando. Do you have an area map?" George took the offered pamphlet, thanked him, and went to the front desk to register for his room. He returned to the bar and told Michael that he requested a room on the fifth floor, the same as the women.

Michael smiled at George's enthusiasm and said, "That's thinking on your feet."

Seated at the desk in his room, Michael studied the photograph of the young contractor that the husband suspected of cavorting with his wife. It wouldn't be hard to spot the good-looking curly-haired man with a burn scar on his left hand. So far, Michael hadn't seen him.

Michael joined his brother downstairs. George had followed Pennington and her friends to the restaurant and was seated not far from the group where he was able to take covert photos. The women left after their meal and went directly to their rooms. Overall, the evening was uneventful.

Their routine was similar for the next few days. Breakfast delivered to one room for the four of them, an early swim, change of clothes, take off for area attractions, dinner at the hotel, and dancing and drinks at nearby clubs.

Michael had taken scores of photos but had yet to see anything to substantiate the husband's claim of his wife's affair with the contractor. He started to think that Pennington was nothing more than she appeared; a thirty-something who wanted a little time away from her much older husband.

It was day five of the investigation. Two of the friends checked out of the hotel at noon. Pennington and one of the women remained. They spent the day lounging in the sun and kept the poolside waiter busy delivering rounds of Mojito's.

A change of their routine in the evening piqued Michael's interest. The women drove to a vineyard, thirty miles away where they spent a couple of hours sampling wines then drove to a country music bar.

Positioned within easy eyeshot of the women, Michael was able to take a clear video and sound of Pennington and her friend in a nearby booth. A couple of clean-cut cowboy types approached the women and were quickly rebuffed.

The more the women drank the closer they sat, and the more ear whispering went on. Then something unexpected caught Michael's attention. Pennington reached her left hand toward her friend and was sure to keep it low then slid her hand up her friend's thigh. Even though the club lighting was subdued, Michael caught on video the subject's hand as she moved it up under her friend's skirt.

While they waited for their check, Pennington slipped her foot out of her shoe and rubbed it on her pal's leg. Michael recorded it, but it wasn't the 'money shot.'

It was one-thirty a.m. when they left the club. Michael was able to slip out and monitor the women. He got a clear video of the two of them playing grab-ass on their way through the lot.

They reached the car, turned to face each other and kissed with unmistakable passion. Michael halted, lifted his 'spy phone' to his ear, leaned against a car and faked a conversation. The women were too engrossed in each other to notice him recording their amorous embrace.

Pennington opened the driver's door for her friend who climbed across the seat, ass up in the air. Pennington scooted in behind her. Michael weaved around parked cars in perfect position to film the women entangled in each other's arms. Pennington was naked from the waist up. The brunette's mouth was on Pennington's bare breast.

Michael got the video he needed and returned to his car where George was stationed with a camera.

"Did you get anything?" George asked with a childlike eagerness.

"Might not be the BIG money shot, but it'll do."

The verbal report Michael gave Connor was to the point. "Unless your client's contractor is a woman, he's looking in the wrong direction. Connor, I've got video and photos. I'll burn it all on a DVD tomorrow and send it to you. Thanks for the work, buddy."

CHAPTER FIVE

The unexpected ring of the phone jolted him from a sound sleep. He looked at the clock. It was eleven p.m. Before he answered, Michael checked the caller I.D. It was Teresa. "Ah, hell."

He answered, "What is it now?"

Half asleep, Michael let her ramble on and spin her story of how her affair with Bill Lang had started and ended, and how she regretted that she had hurt Michael. As she cried, he listened with hostile bitterness while she begged him for another chance and swore she would never again betray him. "Michael, it was a mistake. It will never happen again."

Fully awake and unmoved by her plea, he formed his words with the utmost care to ensure she would understand. Michael choked back tears. "The destruction you caused to my life is irreparable."

In monotone he stated, "You are dead to me."

She gasped.

He continued, "Never contact me again," and hung up.

At last it was over.

He rolled to his side, and for the first time since he moved out of their home, he had a sound sleep.

Michael woke and felt clear and unburdened. Had he known how cathartic it would feel to slam and lock that door permanently with Teresa, he would have said those words to her long ago.

That afternoon, Michael sat at the bar inside Pete & Shorty's, his favorite neighborhood tavern. The pretty young waitress with the over-whitened teeth smiled at him flirtatiously. He ordered his usual burger with seasoned fries and sipped on a beer while he mulled over an offer that Connor had made several times. Michael mentally listed the Pro's and Con's and couldn't come up with any good reason not to make the move to Philadelphia and work with Connor.

Michael knew it would be a great opportunity and had to admit that he was enticed by the offer. He found no good reason to stay in Florida any longer, especially after Connor said, "Michael, I need you."

CHAPTER SIX

Philadelphia, Pennsylvania

Ann Paxton first arrived in Philadelphia in the spring, a time of year that represented renewal, a perfect time to begin her new life.

The transformation from Anne Preston of Florida to Ann Marie Paxton in Philadelphia took some effort but the end result had been remarkable. No one would mistake her for the red-haired Florida psychic, Anne Preston, with the English accent.

Ann Marie Paxton was a natural blonde. It took several attempts before the cosmetologist achieved the perfect shade of blonde to match her roots. It was a stroke of genius to resume her true identity and real social security number which she hadn't used since she left Ohio.

She was fortunate that she was able to lease office space on Walnut Street within walking distance of her apartment on Rittenhouse Square. The office was more than suitable to attract the high-end clientele she desired for her psychic counseling business. The dark blue Lexus she leased was the finishing touch to her image.

It had taken months for her business to grow enough to support her comfortable lifestyle. Ann's reputation for accuracy with her readings ensured a steady flow of people who sought her advice. She no longer had to tap into the cache of money she brought with her from her office in Florida. She felt it ridiculous to pay taxes on the cash she received and thought it prudent to declare only enough income sufficient to cover her expenses. For most purchases, it was her habit to pay with cash to prevent those transactions from being tracked.

It was a bright Fall morning, crisp and clear. Ann liked the fact that she could walk to work on these days. In her office, she slipped out of her walking shoes and into her high heels and made a cup of Earl Grey tea while she waited for her ten a.m. appointment. The neurotic widow was always late. There was a knock on her office door. It wasn't whom she expected. It was a courier there to deliver a package.

She sat on the sofa, put down her cup, and opened the decorative gift box that was from a wealthy client who lived on Mermaid Lane in Germantown. The card inside read:

> Dear Ms. Paxton,
> Please accept this gift as a token of my gratitude for your insightful guidance in reference to my business opportunity in South Africa.
> I must admit the malachite worry stone you gave me has indeed brought good fortune as you stated it would.
> Best Regards,
> GGM

Inside the box was a small antique clock signed René Lalique. Ann noticed the correct time had been set and true to form her first patron of the day was already fifteen minutes late.

Ann went to her desk where she carefully positioned the clock in a prominent place, opened a drawer and slipped the note card inside next to her hot pink stun gun.

Minutes later there was a knock at the door. The session went as it always did. There was nothing remarkable to tell the woman. She had no children, no social life to speak of, she had no health issues, there were no changes to her financial security; she was simply a lonely rich widow who needed someone to talk to and Ann was happy to take her money for the visit.

It was three p.m. before Ann took a break. Her day had been

filled with the usual questions from clients; is my spouse cheating; am I going to get a new job; how is my health? There was no challenge to Ann in working with these people. This was not her mission, but it did provide the financial means to accomplish her life's work.

It wasn't unexpected for a first-timer to withhold their name, but when Ann's last appointment sauntered in wearing oversized sunglasses and dressed like a film noire character, sans trench coat, Ann stifled a laugh. The woman began the session by dictating to Ann that their conversation had to be confidential and that she must have anonymity.

"I can assure you that all of my readings are confidential, and I never disclose the identity of anyone who comes into this office," Ann stated. "You may repeat anything I tell you to anyone you choose, but I do not discuss what I reveal to a client with anyone." *Like I give a shit about your life.*

The woman's hand shook as she removed her designer sunglasses and stuck them in her pocket.

Ann began by stating specific facts of the woman's past that only she would know and moved on to present information.

. . . "The multi-million-dollar malpractice claim that you won for your law firm against University Hospital will be lost on appeal."

. . . "Your husband will be sanctioned but he will not lose his license to practice law. And yes, he is guilty of the offense of which he was charged."

. . . "By this time next year, you will be divorced. If you hope to make a decent settlement, I suggest you hire a forensic accountant right away to find your husband's hidden finances."

The color drained from the woman's face. Her reaction was to the significant financial loss rather than the emotional loss of her marriage.

Ann knew that if the shyster's wife did as Ann advised, she would land on her feet. She handed her a citrine worry stone. "When you feel the need, hold the stone. The energy of the citrine will assist you in making clear, informed decisions."

Ann concluded the hour long reading with, "In sixteen months your life will be changed in every way."

On the way out of Ann's office, the woman resumed her affected identity as a femme fatale character in a 1940's movie.

Weary but satisfied after a long and profitable day, Ann took her day's receipts, all cash, from the safe that was camouflaged as an ornamental chest and closed and locked the office door behind her. She savored the beautiful Fall weather on her walk home. The colors of Indian Summer reminded her of Ohio and her walks to school with her foster-sister Jane, and the ginger cookies their foster-mother, Florence, had ready for them when they returned home. It was a rare, nice memory from a lifetime ago.

Something in the window of the bookstore near Ann's office caught her eye. She stopped at once. A book, <u>Psychic Awareness</u> by Allison Rogers-DeMarcou was on display. Ann hurried inside to make her purchase.

She hoped she wasn't mentioned in the book. Ann sat on a bench under a huge sycamore tree in Rittenhouse Square across from her apartment and scanned the Glossary for her name. It wasn't listed. On the inside cover was a photo of Allison Rogers along with her bio. *That interfering troublemaker is married . . . living in Clearwater, Florida.*

Ann closed her eyes and tilted her head to feel the late afternoon sun on her face. It wasn't that long ago that she enjoyed the warmth of the sun from her balcony in Clearwater that overlooked the Gulf of Mexico. She was comfortable with the life she had created there. If Allison Rogers had minded her own damn business, and Elliott Gelman hadn't become obsessed with Ann and forgot that it was she who was in charge of the missions, she might have stayed in Florida.

She tucked the book under her arm and started across the street toward her apartment when a horse-drawn carriage, replete with a driver in an historical costume, ferried two enormously obese people in front of her. They reminded her of oompah loompahs.

She felt pity for the horse.

CHAPTER SEVEN

Ann entered Scarpetta, the restaurant located on the ground floor of her apartment building and was greeted by the maître d' when she entered. "Good evening, Ms. Paxton." Kurtz escorted her to the table in the corner, next to the window. "I'll have your waiter bring your glass of sauvignon blanc." Ann found his energy welcoming. He was dignified with an air of old world charm.

She sipped on her favorite white wine, gazed at the pedestrian traffic outside the window, and immediately recognized the couple who approached the restaurant. She had seen them in the dining room on a number of occasions. The woman resembled a young Anne Hathaway. The man reminded her of George Clooney; fit and distinguished.

A clatter of dishes that crashed to the floor caused heads to turn and a red-faced waiter and a busboy scurried to clean up the mess. Ann glanced back and saw the same man and woman with the movie star looks enter the room. From their body language, it didn't take a psychic to know that they were lovers, but the intuitive part of Ann knew that he was married, but not to the young woman. The energy exchange between them was a deep passion.

She turned her head away from the oddly uncomfortable scene and stared out of the window. She reflected on how different her life would have been had she had that kind of infatuation with someone. The charade of her disingenuous romance with Tim McMullen, a long-distance trucker, didn't count. He was only a vehicle to get her away from her waitress job at the truck stop and away from Ohio. It was during a two-day layover in Oregon that Ann slipped out of their motel room before dawn. She stole $800.00 in cash from him, left a note that said, 'thanks for the lift,' and began her new identity as Anna McMullen. That's when she became a chameleon. Anna McMullen would be the first of many aliases.

Her train of thought took Ann back to her horrific childhood. The sound of her cries when she was taken from her abusive mother still resonated within her. She remembered it as if it was yesterday, being put into the child welfare system and assigned to a deeply religious family.

As an adult, she understood that some of what happened in her young life was because she was different. She was born with the ability to see events before they happened and knew private things about people. Her new foster-parents, 'Aunt' Josie and 'Uncle' Bob, soon discovered that she could tell them about their secrets.

After four years of bible study that she was forced to attend to rid her of her unnatural affliction, she figured that if she told her foster-parents that the angels gave her the information like they did the prophets, that she wouldn't be punished anymore.

Ann stared at her reflection in the restaurant window. She re-called when she told her Aunt Josie not to be sad about the little girl she gave away when she was in high school and that if she wanted, Ann would be her little girl. Ann thought that would make Aunt Josie happy. Instead, she screamed at Ann calling her an evil liar, locked her in the small hall closet, and ordered her to pray for forgiveness, for what, she wasn't sure. It was the next morning before Ann was allowed out of the tight space only after she promised to never tell anyone that terrible lie.

Desperate to be accepted and loved, Ann tried to be helpful. She had a vision about the church pastor and warned him that he would soon die. Her revelation was received as another one of her tall tales. At the conclusion of Sunday services, Ann was brought up in front of the congregation by the pastor and scorned as a dreadful child who would say or do whatever she wanted to get attention and that she must repent.

She cried, "I hate you!" and ran from the church.

His death happened within the month. The pastor was on vacation in Kentucky when his vehicle got stuck on railroad tracks and was struck by a coal train. He was trapped inside. Congregants of the church believed Ann caused the accident.

She overheard Aunt Josie and Uncle Bob talking to a church deacon at the funeral service for the pastor. The deacon told them that the congregation was afraid of Ann and believed she was the spawn of Satan.

She was only a little girl and didn't know what spawn meant, but she knew it wasn't good.

Ann took a sip of wine and shuddered as she recalled the day she returned home from school and was met by Aunt Josie, Uncle Bob, and a group of church elders who escorted her straight to the dining room where all the drapes were drawn closed. They secured her arms and legs to a chair and for hours she endured what she later learned was their attempt at an exorcism.

The extreme treatment came to the attention of law enforcement through the concern of a neighbor who overheard the forceful adult voices and the screams of a terrified child. The ritual ended when the police stormed inside the house and cut her free from her restraints. Safe and protected in the company of a female officer, she watched from the patrol car as one by one the adults who had assaulted her filed out of the house and were put into a police van. She could still see Aunt Josie's tear-streaked face and the hatred in the eyes of Uncle Bob as he gave her a look that would kill when he walked past the car in handcuffs.

The new home where Ann had been placed, was clean, cheerful, and there was only one other child in residence. The little girl, Jane, had lived in that home months before Ann got there. Ann was struck by Jane's big, brown eyes that were filled with sadness, in contrast to the beauty of her face and jet-black braids that made her resemble an Indian princess. It was Jane's gentle personality and innocence that won Ann's heart. They bonded immediately and began to refer to each other as sisters.

'Aunt Suzie,' her new foster-mother, was kind, pleasant, and a great cook who often allowed the girls to help her make cookies and pies for her Women's Club meetings.

It wasn't long after Ann's arrival that 'Uncle Johnny,' her husband, would come to Ann's room at bedtime, kiss her on the forehead, and wish her sweet dreams. There was something about him that gave her the creeps. She wasn't comfortable with what she supposed was a fatherly gesture.

What started out as an innocent goodnight kiss turned into a nightly horror. The two girls never spoke about Uncle Johnny's behavior, but Ann knew she wasn't the only one he visited in the darkness. She understood the look of misery she saw in Jane's eyes. It was for Jane's sake and her own that Ann stood up to their lecherous guardian, Uncle Johnny.

The same surge of vengeance that motivated her that day when she hid behind the open cellar door and held her breath, coursed through her as she remembered the events.

Ann shuddered at her intense reaction to the memories and took a big gulp of her wine.

She recollected the tone of his voice and knew what it meant when she heard Uncle Johnny call her name and unzip his pants. She pictured the day she tip-toed out from where she hid behind the basement door and came up behind him. She felt his sweaty back against her palms and the force it took for her to push him, hard, as the bastard tumbled down the cellar stairs with his pants undone, his broken body at the foot of the steps.

She caught her breath recalling the empowerment she experienced when she raised the shovel and saw the terror in his eyes as she smashed it on his head.

He'd never rape another little girl. She knew then that it was her destiny to protect the innocent, to guarantee that the guilty were punished.

Uncle Johnny was the first.

"Uh hmm," the waiter cleared his throat. "Are you ready to order now, Ms. Paxton?"

"Oh. . .yes." She gave her order.

The waiter turned away with military precision. Ann was amused by his pretentious gesture until she caught sight of the 'handsome' couple across the room. Again, she thought about her life. She could never imagine having that intimacy with any man.

No, her life was bound to the innocent, to those who were wronged, and to those who were not punished for their crimes against the vulnerable.

CHAPTER EIGHT

Michael's move to the City of Brotherly Love to work with Connor, went without a hitch. Although he had a little trepidation of how this change in his life would suit him, he was optimistic.

He stood outside of Society Hill Investigations. The building was made with glazed bricks in muted colors that ranged from pink to orange-red. Connor told him that the structure was once used as a firehouse in Colonial days. Michael pictured the volunteer firemen with leather buckets slung over their shoulders and imagined them pulling the water wagon to a fire.

A sudden pat on his shoulder caught Michael off-guard. "Good morning," Connor greeted him. "Welcome to your new digs."

With a tour of the building and introductions to staff out of the way, Michael entered his office. He was impressed by the collection of timeworn photographs of historic firetrucks that were hung on the original brick wall of his office. He tried to imagine how the early firemen were able to extinguish a blaze with their primitive equipment. Michael had a newfound appreciation for the history of the old firehouse.

#

His comfort level from the first day he stepped into his office, amazed him. It felt as if this was where he was meant to be. Connor was right about there being more work than his staff could handle. Enthusiastic and motivated, Michael jumped in with both feet.

At Connor's insistence, Michael moved into the spare bedroom in Connor's home while he searched for his apartment. He insisted Michael could stay as long as he wanted. They spent most evenings discussing cases, watching the Sports Network, or talking about Michael's dad. Their relationship became closer than most fathers and sons.

The older man ran his home like he ran his office—military style. There was a right way and a wrong way to do everything. Michael was no slob, but he wouldn't miss seeing Connor spit shine his shoes before he went to bed.

Michael cared for and respected Connor, but he knew he'd soon have to have his own home, where, if he wanted to leave his bed unmade or his laundry in a pile, he could and not feel guilty.

#

It took Michael a full day to make his way through the furniture store on Spruce Street. By the time he was done, he had picked out all that he needed to furnish his new apartment from top to bottom. Michael liked having his own place and although he didn't think he would, he had to admit he missed Connor's quirky routines.

The men made it a point to eat at least one meal together every week. They'd shoot the shit about work, talk about the old days with Michael's dad, and no matter the topic, Connor would always end the meal reminiscing about Betty. The persistent cough Connor had concerned Michael especially since his friend seemed disinclined to pay the doctor another visit. "What's the worst that can happen?" he'd say. "I'll get to be with my sweet Betty again."

A heavy workload kept Michael busy with cases that routinely took him into the diverse neighborhoods that made up Philadelphia and surrounding areas. For him, being a P.I. had all the challenges and excitement of law enforcement without the stringent rules of the department.

CHAPTER NINE

The awning of the closed hoagie shop on Front Street gave shelter to the huddled person backed into the doorway. The shadowed figure tugged on the drawstring that tightened the hood of the sweatshirt, but it did little to fend off the cold rain blowing in from the Delaware River.

An imposing silhouette of a man half a block to the south stepped out of the plumbing supply store and locked the door. He reached up and lowered the rusted metal grate to secure the storefront, flipped up the collar of his rain coat, and cupped his hand at his forehead to shield his glasses from the rain. The man walked north in the direction of the hoagie shop, stumbled over a box of trash left on the sidewalk and cursed the punks who shot out the street lamp again.

The hooded figure under the awning stepped onto the sidewalk into the rain, walked in the direction of the lumbering man, and when they were a few feet apart, aimed a gun at the big man's crotch, fired twice, dropped a typed note next to the body, and continued down the sidewalk.

Across the street in the alleyway was a car with an occupant illuminated only by the light of a cellphone.

Within minutes, police and rescue responded to the 9-1-1 call. Blood mixed with rain spread across the concrete and ran into the gutter. A driver's license and business card found on the victim identified him as James Bakker, owner of Bakker Plumbing Supply. He had bled out from gunshot wounds that mutilated his genitals and severed the femoral artery. The hysterical witness described to police the flashes of light she saw and two pops she heard. She stated she didn't get a good look at the assailant who wore a dark hoodie. The witness told police that the shooter 'just strolled away' in the direction of the waterfront.

#

The black hooded sweatshirt and the water-soaked Doc Martin's were removed and left on the mat in the foyer. In the bedroom on the cedar chest positioned at the foot of the bed, an outline of a damp naked ass remained on the polished surface along with a pair of wet panties.

Relaxed in the tub and surrounded by lavender scented candles she grinned as she remembered the bewildered expression on the degenerate pig's face as the revolver fired, the sound of the thud when the despicable heap collapsed on the ground, the relief she felt when the gun still loaded with three hollow-point bullets, splashed into the Delaware River . . . thoughts of her accomplishment gave rise to distant memories of punishment and making those pay who thought they got away.

The legal system's blind eye was flawed beyond words but, she was satisfied that the scales of justice were now balanced. She whispered, "You can barricade your store and padlock the grate, but you can't protect yourself from me. That was your karma for what you did to Claudette."

#

Seated in the bistro with a large latte in hand, she searched the Philadelphia Enquirer for any report of last night's event. She found it on Page 2.

James Bakker, 62, the owner of Bakker Plumbing Supply on Front Street, died of multiple gunshot wounds outside of his store late Friday night. A police spokesman stated that robbery did not appear to be the motive. Witnesses reported a small statured male in a dark hooded jacket leave the scene on foot.

Bakker was a person of interest in the rape and murder of his nineteen- year- old niece, Claudette Tyler, who had Down Syndrome. Ms. Tyler, who wandered away during a family picnic at Fairmount Park, was later discovered by her uncle, James Bakker.

As of this date, there have been no arrests. Anyone with information related to the murder of Claudette Tyler or James Bakker should contact the Philadelphia Police Department.

Amused that she was described as a 'male in a hoodie,' she finished her cappuccino, folded the paper, tucked it under her arm and returned home where she cut out the article, wrote across the headline, 'Paid in full,' and slipped it in with the other clippings.

CHAPTER TEN

Forced to endure the abuse of church elders when she was a child, Ann Paxton had never succumbed to any religious doctrine. She believed only in the law of karma. Sunday held no religious meaning, yet it was the one day of the week that Ann kept her schedule unstructured. She indulged herself and only herself. No whining clients, no one demanding her precious advice, no work in any way.

On this cool Sunday morning, Ann walked through Rittenhouse Square, her intent to get English tea and a scone across from her building at the quaint café she discovered soon after her move to Philadelphia. As soon as she entered she recognized a diminutive elder man whom she often noticed reading on a bench in the park. She was impressed by his appearance; a shock of white hair, impeccably dressed. He reminded her of a gentleman from another era.

He smiled and greeted her with a courteous wave. She returned the smile, nodded 'hello,' and followed the hostess who seated her in quiet section in the back of the room. She sat alone content to enjoy a leisurely morning. The simple white vase with a single rose on the table was a lovely touch.

Her order came, and Ann scooped the clotted cream onto her scone. She was ready to take a bite when the older gentleman walked up to her and said, "Please excuse the intrusion."

Her solitude interrupted, she asked, "May I help you?"

"Allow me to introduce myself. I am Franklin Carroll. As we continue to see one another on our walks through the square, it occurs to me that we may be neighbors." He extended his hand to Ann. "And you are?"

She reluctantly offered her hand to him. "I am Ann Paxton. And yes, we may very well be neighbors."

"Very nice to meet you, indeed," Franklin said, and leaned into a slight bow. "And now that we are acquaintances, I hope the next time we see one another here, you will feel comfortable in joining me."

"Perhaps," Ann replied, with no intention to accept his offer.

"Good afternoon, Ms. Paxton." Franklin smiled and left the café.

The waitress returned to refill Ann's cup. "I see you know Judge Carroll," she said with a pleasant smile. "He's such a nice man. Wasn't it terrible what they said about him on television the other day, just for letting that guy out of jail early?"

"I know nothing about him. We've just met." *So much for my peaceful morning.* "May I have the check please?"

CHAPTER ELEVEN

The quiet drone from the television reporter on KYW filled the room with background noise. "James Bakker . . . plumbing supply . . . waterfront." Michael looked at the television too late to catch the full story. An attractive meteorologist pointed to a weather system that was predicted to linger for the rest of the week.

Michael made his second cup of coffee and carried it to the sofa, opened his laptop and read the background report about the waterfront job that he would start in the morning, made a few notes, and turned off the computer. At first light tomorrow, he'd head to a pier off Delaware Avenue to find out, if possible, who, how, and why, recent excessive thefts of electronics were so prevalent from cargo ships at that one particular dock.

In an unsecured lot outside of the gate to the pier, Michael rechecked the equipment, and set the video camera on the dashboard aimed at the entrance gate. Employees' bags and gear were checked upon entrance and exit through the gate. At the end of the day, Michael had observed two guards on each shift, morning and afternoon. He did a double-take when he realized the massive physique on one of the morning shift guards, belonged to a female who gave the impression she could easily bench press her tall lanky male co-worker.

On the second day of the surveillance, the security routine appeared to be unchanged. Stevedores and other workman passed through the gate as they entered and exited the pier and with an obligatory gesture opened their parcels. The guards gave a disinterested nod and waived them through. Michael noticed one side of the entrance was used for everyone.

He took note that over the last couple of days a specific group of five burly longshoremen, who carried obviously full duffle bags out at the end of their shifts, were waved through the checkpoint with a cursory glance into the open bag. The same guards were on duty, the same workers each time. Michael watched the men climb into two separate pickup trucks that sat side by side and pull away. One of the vehicles had a large distinctive emblem on the driver side door. It was a green eagle flying through goal posts with a football in its talons. *Another rabid Eagle's fan.*

At sunrise the next morning, Michael showed up in a different company vehicle to disguise his presence and ensure he wouldn't be detected.

The five men he had been keeping an eye on the day before, drove up in the same two trucks within minutes of each other. They walked to the gate. Each carried a large folded gym bag tucked under their arm which they gratuitously opened for inspection. Michael waited until they walked down the length of the pier before he drove to their respective vehicles, took pictures of the pickups including the tags, and through the windows took photographs of the interiors. A baseball bat was on the floor of the back seat of the Eagles fan's truck.

Throughout the morning, Michael kept an attentive eye on the gate and the vehicles. By mid-afternoon, his bladder felt like a basketball. He took a quick bathroom break at a nearby convenience store, bought a candy bar, and returned to his position. The shift ended, and a surge of bodies left the pier. Three of the five men he had been watching came through the gate. They carried what now appeared to be full, heavy gym bags, and drove out of the lot. There was no sign of the other two men. Except for the guards, the pier was empty.

Michael waited.

A sudden feeling of uneasiness caused the hair on the back of his neck to bristle. He glanced into the rearview mirror and saw the two men approach his vehicle with rapid intent, baseball bats in hand.

"Shit!" Michael started the engine and hauled ass with a squeal of tires. Papers flew on the floor. The camera slid across the dash. Instinctively, Michael grabbed for it but missed. He looked out of the side window and saw the female guard. She laughed and gave Michael the finger.

Seated at his kitchen table that evening, Michael opened his laptop and wrote his report. It was obvious that 'someone' didn't want him to see what was going down at the pier. Whatever it was, it had danger written all over it.

#

The close encounter with the two longshoremen yesterday forced Michael to go to a new location near the pier, and in a different car. It was mid-day when the driver of the 'green eagle' truck who came at Michael yesterday with the baseball bat, pulled out of parking lot, alone.

Michael tailed him to Bazzini's, a south Philadelphia restaurant and a suspected organized crime hangout. He drove past the building and stopped behind a work van on the opposite side of the street. There he sat for hours and recorded anyone who entered or exited the establishment.

"Shit." A charley horse knotted his calf into a rock-hard ball of flesh. He tried to rub it out, but it didn't help much. Michael tucked the camera under the seat, jumped out of the car and limped to the sidewalk to stretch out the muscle. Without warning, a strong hand gripped his shoulder like a vice and spun him around.

Michael was eye to eye with a bald-headed Goliath. "Whoa man," he held up his hands, "I don't want any trouble." There was no time to react to the massive fist that connected with his face. Agonizing pain ripped through Michael's jaw. He went down hard onto the sidewalk and was kicked in the ribs. He lay in a fetal position and tried to gasp air back into his lungs.

The assailant grabbed Michael's shirt collar and dragged him to the driver's side of his car. "Get your ass up, fuckhead. You don't know who you're messin' with. Stop pokin' around and get the fuck outta here. Don't let me see your face again."

Michael stood, unsteady on his feet, and leaned on the car for support. He opened the door, braced himself with his left hand on the door frame, and lowered himself into the car.

"Don't 'cha let me see your fuck'n face around here again." The thug slammed the door on Michael's left hand and sauntered away.

"Oh God!" Michael shoved the door open with his shoulder, turned his body and puked into the gutter, cold sweat dripped from his forehead. He held his injured hand close to his body. With his good hand, Michael unbuttoned his shirt, wriggled his right arm out of the sleeve, and wrapped his bloody left hand.

#

"Do I really need to fill this paperwork out now?" Frustrated and in pain, Michael shoved his driver's license and insurance card toward the Emergency Room attendant.

"Mr. Vega, please take a seat. Someone will be with you soon."

In the crowded ER, Michael was surrounded by people in various stages of illness and apparent discomfort. A couple of hyper little boys ran around the room. A three- hundred-plus-pound woman threatened to knock the crap out of them if they didn't sit down. "I told you to behave. I don't feel good." A homeless man walked in and demanded to see a doctor; a heavy cloud of shit smell emanated from the derelict.

Michael couldn't stand the wait or the chaos and stood to leave. He'd find a walk-in clinic somewhere.

"Mr. Vega," an attractive nurse dressed in purple scrubs called out and scanned the room.

"Right here," Michael winced from the pain in his swollen jaw.

She escorted him to a treatment room, assisted him on to a bed, and asked, "How did this happen?"

Michael explained to the pretty nurse that he was beat up by a little old lady he tried to help cross the street.

The nurse raised an eyebrow, shook her head, and said, "Mr. Vega, let me take a look at that." The nurse cut the wrapped shirt away from his hand. "Let's get you cleaned up. Dr. Mara will be right with you."

Michael laid on the bed, his eyes focused on the ceiling, angry for making a rookie mistake. He waited for what seemed an eternity before the doctor returned with the results from the X-rays. "You're a lucky man, Mr. Vega. Nothing's broken but your jaw and ribs are badly bruised. You're going to have to stick with soft foods for a couple of days. We're going to stitch up that hand, give you antibiotics, and get you on your way."

Michael cringed at the thought of stitches.

"That wasn't so bad now, was it Mr. Vega?" the nurse said as the doctor left the room.

"Only because you held my good hand," Michael teased.

"I'll be right back with your discharge papers. Now, don't go away." She returned with his paperwork and handed him a scrub top. "Mr. Vega, you'll need something to wear home." She started to read the aftercare instructions to him.

Her intense blue eyes were framed by long black lashes. How had he missed those eyes? Under normal circumstances that would have been the first thing he saw. This was anything but normal. He read her badge. Meg B., RN.

"What if the pain gets really bad when I'm home all alone?" Michael said playfully.

"Come on, Mr. Vega. A big, strong man like you doesn't have anyone to look after him?"

Michael liked the way this conversation was going. "Nope. Like I said, I'm all alone." Their banter continued a little longer before he asked if she'd like to have dinner with him sometime.

"I really can't–"

"Well, can I at least have your phone number?"

"No, but I have yours," she smiled and walked out of the room.

He left the hospital with a grin on his face and her name on his mind. *Meg B., RN.*

CHAPTER TWELVE

Michael stood at the stove and struggled to make himself something to eat. He'd already dropped an egg on the floor and watched the slime run under the range. "Damn." His hand throbbed, he hadn't slept much, and his jaw hurt like he went six rounds with Rocky Balboa. He bent to clean up the mess and felt as if every rib cracked in half. "Mother f—," his yell was interrupted by the ring of the phone.

"Vega," he barked.

"Good morning, Mr. Vega. This is Meg Burnside the nurse from University Hospital. I called to check on you and how you're feeling, but I believe I just got my answer."

Embarrassed at his abruptness, Michael tried to pull himself together and come up with a witty response but couldn't.

Meg continued, "I remember you said you were all alone . . ."

His conversation with Meg made him forget how lousy he felt and by the end of the call, Meg had agreed to have dinner with him, but on her terms. She would stop by after work and bring food.

Meg was at the front door at six p.m. on the dot with a picnic basket filled with food and headed right for the kitchen. She gave him orders to stay in the living room and rest, while she took care of dinner. Their casual talk while they ate homemade soup became more personal after cake and ice cream. He learned a lot about her large close-knit Irish family; she had never been married but had ended a long-term relationship a year ago; she had a twelve-year career in nursing that she loved; they shared a dislike of opera, broccoli, and vampire movies, but had a mutual love of football,

50

albeit not the same teams. Michael was willing to overlook that flaw.

It blew his mind at how comfortable he was with her. They agreed that it felt like they had known each other for a long time. Before either one noticed, it was early morning.

Weekend plans made, Meg kissed Michael's cheek and said goodbye at the door.

Michael grinned like a schoolboy on his first date. *That bald-headed Goliath yesterday did me the biggest favor.*

CHAPTER THIRTEEN

The faded scar left on Michael's hand from his encounter with *Goliath* and the car door, was a reminder of how dangerous his job could be. His position with Connor allowed him to work like a cop, but without all the bullshit restrictions of political correctness, and without the authority of a badge.

Life was good for Michael. He had Meg in his life, he and Connor had forged an unbreakable bond as close as father and son, the business continued to expand, and additional employees were hired. Michael's biggest concern was that Connor had lost more weight over the last couple of months. He wasn't about to broach the issue since Connor made it clear the last time that his health was a closed subject. Besides, Connor called to say he had something important to discuss and wanted to meet for lunch. Maybe he had gone to the doctor after all. Michael could only hope.

The diner was a classic 1950's restaurant replete with a jukebox, and a waitress who wore a white ruffled apron, her bright red hair in a bouffant. She recognized Michael from his weekly meals there with Connor. "Hi doll, your friend's waiting for you." She motioned in the direction of where Connor was seated.

From across the diner, Michael was disturbed to see how frail his good friend looked.

"Good to see you," Connor's voice sounded raspy and weak. "You doin' okay?"

Michael slid into the booth. "Yepper."

"How's it going with you and that pretty nurse of yours?"

Michael attempted to sound nonchalant but couldn't hide his smile. He talked about Meg until the waitress interrupted.

"Bring you boys the daily special? It's super good today. I promise you'll love it."

Both men nodded and laughed as she moved to a couple seated at the counter and ask the same question with the same perkiness. Michael joked that she must receive a commission on each corned beef and cabbage special she sells.

"Your hand feeling better?" Connor asked.

Michael flexed his fingers, "It's doing okay. But, if I see the bastard again, I'll slam his dick in a car door and see how he likes it."

Connor shuddered. "And since we're on the subject of dicks, I'm sorry you won't have that opportunity. Let me update you. I turned over all the evidence you collected on that job to the client. The last picture you took before you got the shit kicked out of you was the money shot. Looks like we pulled out of the waterfront job at the right time. Two of the guards and five stevedores have been arrested. The female guard is throwing everybody under the bus to save her own ass. It was a well-organized theft ring. The Feds are involved now."

Connor handed Michael an envelope. "Here's your bonus."

Michael looked inside at the check. "Holy shit."

"You earned it, son."

Michael felt Connor's gaze and looked at him. There was a serious expression on the older man's face.

"Michael, I've got something important to discuss with you and I ask you not to say anything until I've finished." Connor reached for a folder in the briefcase he had on the seat. "You know I love you like the son I never had, and God knows I respected your dad who always had my back."

"Where're you going with this?"

"Hold on. Here." Connor slid the manila file to Michael. "Open it."

Inside the folder Michael found copies of paperwork pertaining to the ownership transfer of Society Hill Investigations to him. Michael sat in stunned silence.

"Michael?"

"I don't get it." Michael's heart pounded.

"I got tired of your nagging," he winked, "and went to the doctor. He says I've got stage four small cell lung cancer and its metastasized. At most, I might have six months."

A sob caught in Michael's throat. He reached across the table for Connor's hand.

"What about a second opinion?"

"Forget it Michael, I've have three, second opinions. I just gave you the best one."

"There has to be something we can do, Connor."

"Michael, let it be. It is what it is." The old man cleared his throat. "Now, let me finish. I have some properties and investments that will go to Betty's shit-for-brains nephew. I'm only doing that for her sister's sake. Anyway," he sighed, "the building and the business are yours. There's enough money in the bank account to keep it going and a big chunk of that is because of you."

Michael struggled to hold back tears but failed.

"Get a grip, son," Connor said with a wry smile, "I'm not dead yet."

#

Connor's death came quickly. A devastated Michael stood at Connor's gravesite and wished he had had more time with him. The Holy Cross Cemetery was bright with sunshine in stark contrast to the darkness that weighed heavy on Michael's heart. Connor would have been humbled by the large number of people who had turned out for his funeral and the sad, funny, and poignant eulogies given by so many attendees.

Connor's long-time friend, Father Madden, ended the service with, "And now he's in heaven with his beloved Betty."

#

Michael got to the office before dawn, not ready to claim Connor's reserved space, he parked in another spot and walked toward the old converted firehouse.

He entered the stillness of the building and walked to the office that Connor had once occupied and insisted Michael use as his own. The faint smell of Connor's cigar smoke lingered in the room. He took the lighter that was shaped like a derringer from the bookshelf and set it on his desk. It was a gift his father had given Connor in the 1950's.

He stared at the lighter. Tears streamed from his eyes.

CHAPTER FOURTEEN

Jane Mara loved this city, the ethnic restaurants, the museums, and the history. Most precious to her was the peace she felt on her strolls through the public park at Rittenhouse Square, a routine she began years ago when her volunteer work at the county health clinic brought her downtown. Her life in Philadelphia was a far cry from her piteous childhood in Ohio. She didn't dwell on her life as a foster-child, but time had not healed the pain she felt whenever she thought of Scarlett. She shivered and wrapped the Pashmina shawl tighter around her when she remembered how she suffered at the hand of the evil bastard Thurman, the chain and cinder block, the bloody mess of Scarlett's delivery and death—and Jane's immeasurable satisfaction from knowing the inferno she started consumed Thurman's wretched body for what he had done.

It was difficult for her to believe that life could have changed so dramatically for her. She thanked the universe every day for the life she had with her husband, Gary. He was brilliant, a respected emergency room doctor, handsome, and charming. She loved him dearly.

It was a beautiful Saturday morning as Jane strolled along the flower-lined path through the grounds. Sunbeams filtered through the trees, vendors sold fruits and vegetables, artisans greeted passersby in hopes of a sale, folk art in various forms lined the square. A Jerry Garcia look-alike played Bird Song on his guitar. A middle-aged couple seated on a bench swayed in rhythm with the music.

A neon green Frisbee flew past Jane and landed on the lawn near a little boy about six years old that she had seen there on several other occasions. Today, he sat alone on the corner of a faded quilt as if he would be swallowed up and die if he touched another part of the fabric. The child's eyes were gloomy, and he was far too reflective for someone so young. His attention was on the young teenaged girl who ran up to retrieve the green disc. She spoke to the boy then flipped the Frisbee back toward the two adults who waited nearby.

Jane strolled closer to the child on the blanket, removed her wrap, spread it out on the grass, and sat near him. He was gaunt and pale. His beautiful blue eyes were underscored by dark circles. Tufts of blonde hair stuck out from under his Phillies ball cap.

"What a beautiful day," Jane said. "My name's Jane. What's yours?"

The child hesitated. "I'm . . . Zack."

"I've seen you here before, Zack."

"I saw you, too, the last time I was here. You gave peanuts to the squirrels."

Jane thought it remarkable when he told her he was eight, a few years older than he appeared. He seemed to be apprehensive, of what she didn't know. She recognized in him the telltale signs she saw in some pediatric patients who came to the clinic; sad eyes and a troubled expression.

"I saw you sitting here all alone. I thought I'd keep you company, if you don't mind."

"I'm not really alone." He pointed to the teen and the two adults. "That's my family, right over there."

"How come you're not playing Frisbee with them?"

"My dad's girlfriend, Gloria, won't let me. That's her with my father and sister. She says I'm too clumsy and told me to sit right here and not move."

"You know what? When I was your age, I was clumsy too. I could trip over a blade of grass." Her comment elicited a slight smile from the boy.

The tinkle of a bell announced the arrival of an ice cream vendor who pushed his cart nearby.

"I could go for an ice cream," Jane said. "Would you like something? My treat."

"No, thank you. I'm only allowed to eat what Gloria fixes for me. It's okay, though. I'm not very hungry anyway."

She hurt for this sweet little boy, started to speak but stopped. Fear covered Zack's face. His eyes widened. He clamped his jaw shut. Jane turned to see what had caught his attention. 'Gloria,' a twenty-something woman, dressed in a tight camo t-shirt and short shorts, ran toward them. Her eyes blazed with anger.

"Zack! Didn't I tell you not to talk to strangers? Get up. We're going home." The woman glared at Jane as if she were a perverted monster about to kidnap her child, jerked Zack's arm and forced him down the walk. He stammered something incoherent.

"I'm sorry," Jane called to them. "I didn't mean any harm. I was just . . ."

While Zack struggled to keep his balance, his shirt slid up and exposed a large bruise on his prominent ribcage.

Zack's father ran over to the blanket with the young girl close behind. He grabbed the quilt, stared at Jane, and shouted, "What were you doing with my son? You stay the hell away from my kid." He and the girl hurried out of sight.

Dumbfounded, a red-faced Jane sat slack-jawed. *How could they think I would— Will they call the police? . . . maybe I should call them first to explain? . . . but he looked so scared, and that bruise . . . he did look sick, maybe leukemia . . . that would explain his frailness and bruise on his back.*

She began to shake. *Take a breath, Jane. Calm down.*

The couple seated on the nearby bench gawked at Jane with a suspicious glare and continued to do so while she grabbed her scarf off the grass and rushed home.

Thoughts of Zack and the incident today distracted Jane while she prepared Gary's birthday dinner. The park had been a favorite place of hers but after what happened she doubted when or if she would return.

In the dining room, the table was set with china and silver. To please Gary, Jane added the Tiffany wine glasses they received as a wedding gift from his parents. The crystal felt as cold to her touch as his parents' attitude toward her. Her husband told her not to take their coolness personally. His mother and father were 'just that way.' They were intellectuals who didn't show their emotions. Jane knew better.

During one of his parents' infrequent visits, not long after Gary and Jane were married, she overheard them comment to Gary that she was a lovely girl, but they questioned why he didn't marry his former girlfriend, Mary Ellen Overton. "She came from a very good family and could give him children." Jane was devastated when she heard their words and shocked that Gary had shared with them that Jane was unable to conceive. She never told him what she overheard. Ashamed of what had happened to her in Ohio, Jane hadn't revealed the circumstances that surrounded Scarlett's death. He was only aware that Scarlett was stillborn and that after her delivery, Jane required a hysterectomy. She wondered if Gary knew how it came to be, would he have defended her against his parents' unkind remarks.

Jane went to the living room where an assortment of wrapping paper, ribbons, and bows, were stacked on the window bench. Gary would be home in twenty minutes which allowed her time to finish wrapping the Ostrich boots he put on his wish list, a habit he started years ago. She found his wish list demeaning. In the first years of their marriage, it hurt that she had to return the presents she chose for him because he didn't 'care for her tastes.' He insisted the list was logical and it would save her the time and the aggravation of returning gifts. After all, that's the way his parents had done it since they married.

What an awful day. Time to reboot.

She poured herself a glass of brandy at the bar, took a couple of sips, returned to the kitchen and checked the progress of the meal. Everything was right on schedule, except for Gary. He was late even though he promised to be home on time for his birthday dinner. She put in several calls to him. They all went straight into voice mail.

Forty-five minutes after she had turned off the oven, Jane heard the garage door open. Gary walked into the kitchen, dropped his keys

on the counter and noticed that the dining room table was set. "Oh .
. . uh . . . sorry I'm late. The nurses gave me a little birthday party."

"I wish you would have called, Gary." If he heard the disappointment in her voice, he didn't react. "I called your cell, but you
didn't answer."

"I was tied up," he snapped. "There's no need to overact. I'm here
now." He started up the stairs and said, "I'm going to take a quick
shower. I'll be right down. Oh, and Jane, its sufficient to leave one
message. You don't have to keep calling."

Jane clenched her teeth, stomped into the kitchen, let out a loud
sigh, and reheated dinner.

Clean-shaven and showered, Gary returned, sat down and poured
the wine as Jane carried in their filled plates from the kitchen.

Gary gulped his glass of wine and poured another.

"Dinner smells good, Jane. I see you went to a lot of trouble."

"Thank you, Sweetheart. I wanted to make your birthday special.
By the way Gary, did your parents call you for your birthday?"

"Yes." He wiped his mouth with his napkin. "They said to say hello." Gary cut into the roast beef on his plate, frowned, and reached for
the gravy boat. "The meat's a little overcooked, but the gravy should
help."

If you weren't so late . . . "Tell me about your party?"

"It was a party, Jane. People, presents, balloons." He could have
been reciting the alphabet for all the emotion he expressed. "Nothing
out of the ordinary."

"Gary, I had an unusual experience today. It was very unpleasant."

"Uh huh."

"It really upset me, Gary."

"Um hm." He doused the meat again with gravy.

Jane explained what happened today with the little boy named
Zack. Her voice filled with emotion, "I guess I could have reported
them."

"Yeah, maybe." Gary finished the bottle of wine, his attention a
million miles away.

"And then the giant anaconda grabbed the crocodile and they tap danced through the streets."

"What?" Gary pushed away his plate.

"Gary, you haven't heard a single word I've said!" She stood, opened her mouth to elaborate, thought better of it and went into the kitchen for the cake. Jane stifled her frustration as she had learned to do years ago through her experience with Thurman. She counted to ten and took a few deep breaths.

Jane accepted that her husband had more stress and pressures to contend with than other men who had simpler jobs, but it was so hurtful when Gary tuned her out especially when she needed him to listen. Gary told her often that he loved her, and she believed him, but at times he could be so abrupt and self-absorbed. Regardless, it was his birthday and she was determined to make the evening pleasant. Besides, it served no purpose for Jane to make his crankiness an issue. She returned to the dining room with the cake, candles lit, and sang <u>Happy Birthday</u>.

"Make a wish, Gary," she forced a smile and waited for him to blow out the candles. "Did you wish for something spectacular?"

"I wished you would have remembered that I'm counting my carbs. I can't eat this. Why would you tempt me with my favorite cake?" He pushed the whole plate aside. "It was a nice gesture though," he placated.

Jane turned away from him without a word and carried the cake into the kitchen. She scrapped the cake off the plate and into the trash. *Happy Birthday, Gary.*

She stood at the sink, rinsed the butter cream icing and shaved coconut from her hands, and closed her eyes. Tears stained her cheeks as much from frustration as from hurt. She reminded herself that he isn't always like this. There are times when he is so sweet, kind, and romantic.

Early in their relationship, he was proud of her determination to succeed and complimented her on how she overcame so much adversity, worked her way through nursing school, and then graduated at the top of her class to become a registered nurse.

It was within the first few months of her position at University Hospital's Emergency Room that she had seen Gary's authoritativeness with staff and respected him for being a strong leader. But it was those times of gentleness and caring with his patients that made her fall in love with him. Doctors at the hospital respected him, many nurses were enthralled by him, but it was Jane he chose. They married later that year.

Soon after, he insisted she leave nursing and make being his wife her career. It had been painful for Jane to walk away from nursing. She had worked long and hard for her degree and loved her job. But she put Gary's wishes ahead of her own.

It pleased him that she volunteered for charitable causes, as he said, time spent more befitting a doctor's wife.

#

It was a quiet Sunday morning, Gary was out for a jog. In the den, Jane concentrated on her plans for the hospital fundraiser. The silence was broken when Gary came in, sweaty from his run.

"Aw, come on, Jane! Haven't I asked you time and time again not to clutter my room with all your paperwork? You know how disorganization upsets me. This is supposed to be MY space. Please take your stuff and work at your own desk."

"Gary, my desk is upstairs, and my file was here. I didn't expect the few minutes I needed to go through this, would be a problem." She spoke with deliberate calmness, "I'll take this and get out of YOUR room." Jane started to leave when he reached out for her arm.

"Jane, I'm sorry. I didn't mean to bark at you like that. I'm just tired from my run." He snuggled her close to his chest. "Come on, let's sit down and talk for a minute. I know being involved in this project means a lot to you." He kissed the back of her hand. "Tell me how the plans are going."

Happy at his show of interest, she loved this side of him. "The committee decided to have a Sock Hop. I think it's a great idea . . . everyone dressed in Poodle skirts, bobby socks, and saddle shoes . . . a live band." She was ecstatic that Gary was interested. "Sweetheart, I thought maybe you'd—"

"What the hell, Jane? You've got to be kidding me. I thought you were planning a ball or a dinner dance. But a sock hop?" he snickered. "Don't demean yourself by getting involved in something so ridiculous. Aren't you and your committee beyond acting like silly teenagers?" Gary stood. "Don't forget you're a doctor's wife." He started to turn away but stopped. "You know what, don't involve me in any of this, and don't expect me to attend."

Stunned, Jane felt the sting of his words.

"Whatever you do, Jane, remember that your involvements reflect on me. Don't embarrass me."

"I won't embarrass you, Gary." As soon as he walked away, Jane picked up the phone, called the committee chairman at home, and resigned.

CHAPTER FIFTEEN

At the last minute and without explanation, Gary changed his mind and decided they would attend the hospital gala.

Cornered by the Committee Chairman who rattled on about how great the attendance was, how much money they raised, and probed for Jane's reason for resigning, Jane needed a cocktail. She looked for Gary's return from the bar and saw him engrossed in conversation with an attractive dark-haired woman. Jane tried to ignore the intimate glances between the two of them. They were fixated on one another.

Several times during the evening, Gary wandered away from Jane and left her to fend for herself. Later, she found Gary and the same woman together on the terrace involved in a quiet and close conversation far away from the festivities. With a twinge of jealousy, Jane approached them and boldly held out her hand to the woman.

"Hello. I'm Jane Mara, Gary's wife." Jane saw an unmistakable flush on the woman's face. Gary introduced Karen Chapman as his new nurse and explained that she had worked at the hospital for three years but recently joined his team in the E.R. His obvious discomfort confirmed Jane's suspicions.

Inside the ballroom, the band began to play *Goodnight Sweetheart*. "Gary, I think that's our cue." Jane took his hand. "Ms. Chapman, you'll excuse us, won't you?"

\#

Annoyed that Gary was late after he promised they'd spend the evening together, Jane read the same paragraph several times without an inkling of what she'd read, closed the book and put it on the cushion beside her.

Another lonely night. *This is getting old.* She understood his schedule was unpredictable, but of late, it had become excessive. She was certain he was having an affair, and with whom. She wasn't naive. *Constant texting, moodiness, too tired for sex.*

An exhausted Gary entered the room. He plopped into the leather armchair and asked Jane, "What're you doing up at this hour?"

"Really? We had tickets to the theater, remember?"

"Jane, please don't start that shit now. I'm beat."

She mustered the courage she needed, not to ask him about the affair, but to face his answer. At first, Gary appeared amused by her—as he put it—ridiculous insecurity, but after Jane's unrelenting demand for the truth and Gary's litany of denials, he finally confessed to the affair with Karen Chapman. It was five a.m. when his excuses, and Jane's anger and tears, had subsided. It mattered little that Gary swore he would end the affair. Jane's heart was broken.

For weeks, Gary apologized to Jane. He begged her forgiveness, regretted what he had done, and swore it was Jane he loved, that he would rather die than hurt her like this again. He told her that Karen meant nothing to him.

Was she a fool to believe him? It confused Jane that she could still love this man who hurt her beyond comprehension, yet, she couldn't imagine her life without him. She needed to give her husband another chance.

Jane agreed after much pleading from Gary, to take some time away together to try to recapture what they once had.

#

Their trip to Tuscany was filled with hours of therapeutic conversations. Tender moments followed evening walks under a star-filled sky. They bicycled their way through beautiful countryside, held hands on their tours through vineyards, and laughed more than they had in a long while. Their time spent in Italy restored the love the couple had for one another. Jane was shocked when Gary talked about renewing their wedding vows. They returned home with a refreshed commitment and discussed adopting a child.

#

It didn't take long after their return from Italy, that Gary was back in the habit of long days and late nights. Jane had been tempted on more than one occasion to stop by the hospital to surprise him with dinner but knew he'd see through the façade. Her returning insecurities would be obvious. She needed to get a grip on her doubts and convince herself that it was his work that kept him so busy.

#

She had the nightmare again. Flames and smoke—she couldn't breathe. She woke in a cold sweat.

Jane reached for Gary, he wasn't there. The clock read three-ten am. She turned on the lamp and accidentally knocked her tattered book off the nightstand and onto the floor. It lay open to the section where Thurman had torn the pages out to punish her. She pictured the smoke rise from the drum out back as the paper burned . . .

Jane shook her head. She preferred to think about her sister Ann reading the story to her, how they laughed at the old-fashioned way the people spoke, and how Jane made Ann laugh every time she would throw her hands up and squeal, "I don't know nothin' 'bout birthin' babies."

How Jane missed Ann.

Jane picked up the book with care, as if it would crumble with the slightest touch, put it back on the bedside table, and turned out the light.

CHAPTER SIXTEEN

One of the first people who came to see Ann Paxton soon after she opened her office in Philadelphia, was married to an oral surgeon whose practice was in downtown Philly. Mrs. Lobianco must have been a beauty before she had excessive amounts of Botox and filler injected into her now mask-like face. Unlike the majority of Ann's clients, she came more often than necessary but was willing to pay Ann's two-hundred-dollar fee. Ann was happy to acquiesce.

Today, Mrs. Lobianco was seated at the desk opposite Ann and was upset.

"Remember when I saw you the last time, Ms. Paxton, you told me about my seventeen-year-old daughter, Donna? My youngest, the really smart one, the one who started college a year early."

Ann nodded. She needed no reminder.

"You warned me of a danger around her for the next month, specific to her being out after dark on a Friday. I thought that prediction was extreme but so far, you've never been wrong. On those days, I wouldn't allow her to drive beyond sundown and made it a point to keep her busy with the family. But on the last Friday of that month, instead of spending the weekend at home, she insisted she needed to stay on campus with her study group. She lied. She went to a party instead."

Ann knew where this story was going.

"I'm so worried, Ms. Paxton. Donna hasn't been the same since. She asked to take a semester off and wanted to come back home. She barely speaks to anyone in the house. Please can you see what's going on with her?"

67

Ann was struck by the absurdity of the woman's question. "Mrs. Lobianco, you don't need me to answer your question. It should be obvious to you that your daughter was somehow traumatized."

"What are you saying?" Mrs. Lobianco stammered.

"Your daughter has experienced something extremely unpleasant. Her behavior is a classic response to a disturbing event. You should take her to see a doctor."

"I suggested that, but she won't hear of it. Even her father can't make her go." The woman started to sniffle and reached in her purse for a handkerchief. "I need to find out what's wrong. Can I bring her in for a reading?"

"As I said," Ann's voice was more forceful, "she needs to see a doctor. I'm a psychic, not a physician. She's your daughter. You need to be a responsible parent." Aggravated at the woman's parental impotence, Ann added, "And, I don't read for minors."

"She's almost eighteen. I'm sure she'd listen to you, Ms. Paxton. I'll pay you double if you make an exception!"

Ann deliberated, for effect. "Alright, Mrs. Lobianco. I'll do that for you."

"Thank you so much, Ms. Paxton." The woman began to cry but her Botoxed face showed no emotion. Mrs. Lobianco stood to leave and laid the cash payment on the desk in front of Ann. "I can't thank you enough."

The office door closed behind the encouraged woman. Ann picked up the cash and put it inside the safe. "Full price and the client's gone in fifteen minutes."

#

Donna Lobianco, a homely young lady, barely five feet tall and void of any vitality, sat slouched and wide-eyed as she listened intently to Ann.

"Donna, I know coming here to speak with me was difficult

for you. I want you to know that I will not repeat anything we discuss. You're safe here."

The girl lowered her eyes and began to nervously pick at a red mark on her cheek. "I don't know what to say," she whimpered.

"You don't have to say anything. I'll talk. I understand what you're feeling, Donna. It wasn't your fault."

Donna avoided eye contact with Ann and fixated on the desk clock.

"I am aware that you have been assaulted."

Donna stiffened in the seat.

"My initial impression is of your attacker," Ann said.

"I didn't say Trey—"

Ann put her finger to her lips. "Shhh. Allow me to continue, please. I see a young, good-looking man with dark hair. He's tall, athletic, and popular. You liked him and believed he liked you. I can see that he was also your first real boyfriend." Ann slid the box of tissues across her desk to Donna whose tears wet her blemished cheeks. "He chose you because of your naiveté and planned every last detail of how he'd meet you, how he'd befriend you, even how he'd charm you into trusting him." Anger seethed within Ann. "I see what that despicable dog did to you."

Donna tried to smother her sobs with her hands. "How could I have been so stupid?"

"You had no idea what he would do to you. You trusted him. Donna, you must go to the police."

"I won't! I won't! I'd rather kill myself than have anyone else know what happened. I'm sorry I even came here!"

"Donna, do you believe you are his only victim?" Ann poured a glass of water from the carafe on her desk and handed it to the girl who clutched the glass and took a long drink.

There was a deafening silence before Donna uttered, "What an idiot I was. I should have paid attention to the rumors on campus about a girl who accused Trey of rape." Donna's attention focused again on the clock.

"He did rape her, just like he raped you," Ann stated.

"But, I can't go to the police. It's too humiliating." Like the proverbial dam that burst, Donna gushed, "I thought he liked me. He told me I was pretty, and I wanted to believe him. But, I'm not pretty! Oh God!" She covered her face with her hands, "I don't care anymore."

As if struck by an unseen force, a determined calm came over Donna. She lifted her head and squared her shoulders. "Who would believe me, anyway? Do you know who his father is? He owns Browning Construction Company in New Jersey and donates millions to the school. He's a powerful man and Trey doesn't let anybody forget it."

"Donna, the truth has power, too. You need to tell the police."

"But I can't. It was my fault. He asked me to go to his frat house so we could be alone. I could have said no, but I wanted to be there." Donna continued in a tempered voice, "He closed the door to his room and I let him kiss me. Then everything happened so fast. He pushed me on the bed and reached under my dress and tore off my panties. I begged him to stop, that he was hurting me, that I was a virgin!" The words seemed to choke her as she went on. "He said he wouldn't let me play that game with him." Now Donna couldn't stop talking. The words flew out of her mouth like an oral stream of consciousness. "I started to scream, and he shoved my panties into my mouth and held them there with his hand. I couldn't breathe. I thought I was going to die. He—he—raped me!

"After he was done, he made me get dressed. He grabbed me by the back of my neck and whispered in my ear, 'You tell, and I'll kill you.' Then, he opened the door and shoved me out of the room. There were guys in the hallway. Trey winked at me and thanked me for stopping by. The guys laughed when they heard him."

"Donna, I know you're not going to involve the police, but will you at least see a therapist?"

"I can't do that! Trey told me he would kill me if I told anybody!"

"Donna, I promise you, Trey won't hurt you. He is nothing more than a bully and he will back down when he's confronted."

"I said, no! If anybody on campus found out that I turned him in, my life would be over. They'll all hate me." Donna grabbed a tissue and blew her nose. "You have to understand," she stuttered, "I don't have many friends. But, everybody likes him 'cause he's a jock and he gets them drugs." The girl slumped in her chair and lowered her head. "You just don't get it."

"Donna, something must be done, and he has to be stopped."

The reading had been more complex than Ann had anticipated and took longer than the usual hour. Donna's loss of innocence disturbed Ann. It affected her in a way that was personal.

She knew Donna wasn't strong enough to deal with this situation on her own. She would need help; a lot of help.

A casual walk home gave Ann the time to shrug off the drama and depression her clients emanated throughout the day. Bored housewives and brainless toads. *If it wasn't for the money* . . . and then, Donna Lobianco, someone whose life Ann could affect.

She was distracted by the commotion up ahead of her. A group of young people had gathered in front of an old hippie playing Grateful Dead music on his guitar. Coins and dollar bills lay inside his open guitar case. He had positioned himself at an intersection of the sidewalks in the garden forcing Ann to walk in the grass to get around the group. In her peripheral vision, she saw Judge Carroll break free from the onlookers and hurry in her direction.

Crap. She hurried her step and pretended not to hear him when he called out to her. She quickened her pace and was irritated when she heard his voice close behind and had no choice but to acknowledge him.

The out-of-breath judge said, "Hello neighbor. How serendipitous we ran into each other."

"Oh, Judge Carroll, how nice to see you again." Dressed in more casual clothes, his appearance was more youthful than the last time they met, and not as unattractive.

Still a bit winded, the judge said, "I'm having a cocktail party for a few close friends next weekend and would be delighted if you would attend."

"Aren't you considerate to think of me?" Ann faked a glance at the appointment calendar on her phone. "What a pity," she feigned, "I'll be out of town that weekend."

"Well then, I hope you will accept my open invitation to stop by for a glass of wine, any time. I have an extensive wine collection that I believe you may find enjoyable. That's where I live." He gestured to the building across the way. "I'm in apartment 1202."

"I'll remember that, Judge Carroll. Thank you."

"Please call me, Franklin."

Ann smiled. "Yes. Franklin."

CHAPTER SEVENTEEN

Ann closed her umbrella, removed her raincoat inside the lobby doors of her office building, and shook off the excess water. An unexpected crash of thunder startled her. She turned to head for the elevators and discovered Donna Lobianco waiting for her on a near-by bench. Donna's distress was obvious. She jumped to her feet and ran toward Ann.

"I don't have an appointment, but I have an emergency and I don't know what to do." Donna opened her cellphone and held it up for Ann to see. "Look what that psycho has done! If my roommate knew I showed these pictures to anyone, she'd die."

Ann ushered the girl into the elevator and to her office, sat next to her on the sofa, and studied the screen on the phone. The pictures infuriated Ann. An overweight young woman, eyes closed, was naked in a vulgar sexual pose. In another photo, the same girl was spread eagle with a sex toy inserted into her vagina.

"Trey did that to her," Donna said with disgust. "He wanted me to see what he did and texted these pictures to me. This is all my fault. I should have listened to you and called the police when he hurt me."

"You're right, you should have, and you still can."

"No, I can't. My friend threatened to call the police. Trey laughed and dared her to call. He shoved her phone to her face. She saw the pictures he had taken and literally threw up."

Donna flushed, "I should have warned her about Trey when he asked her for help with a computer problem, but I never thought he would hurt her . . . he barely knew her. You know, my roommate's

73

really tech savvy and she helps a lot of people." Donna added, "He even said he'd pay her for her time.

"I never suspected . . .

"She was all messed up when she came back to the dorm. She said the last thing she remembered was sitting at his computer and drinking the Diet Coke he gave her. The next thing she knew she was on the floor, naked and in pain, her underwear wadded in her mouth. She didn't know what happened, then, she saw the blood between her legs. That's when Trey came out of the bathroom. He threw her clothes at her, called her a fat stinking pig, and ordered her to leave.

"He pushed her out into the hall and actually asked her if she would come back if he had more computer issues.

"I didn't want to tell her that he sent those pictures to me, but I had to. You don't think he sent them to anyone else, do you?" she asked, fear in her eyes.

Ann didn't compromise the truth. "I know he sent them to his other victims as a warning."

The color drained from Donna's face. "No, no!"

Ann said, "He sent them from your friend's phone to make sure the other girls would believe his threats."

Donna started to cry and bit her lip. "I can't, I just can't go to the police."

"Well, that's your choice. Stop crying! I told you to go to the authorities. They're the only ones who can help you now. There's nothing more I can do for you."

CHAPTER EIGHTEEN

Loud rock music assaulted her ears before she entered the Eagle's Nest bar. She undid another button on her silk blouse and smoothed the black leather pants over her firm hips. At the top of the steps, a man who wore a green and gray team jacket held open the door. She stepped inside and waited near the entrance until her eyes adjusted to the dim lights. The club was jammed with college students. Several young men turned and nodded their approval. She nodded in turn. One of the bartenders gave her a 'thumbs up.' She acknowledged his gesture with a slight smile.

At the bar, she ordered a Mojito and tossed a fifty-dollar bill on the counter. She scanned the room for the person whose face she had studied on *his* Facebook page. From his post, he was supposed to be here tonight.

The handsome buff bartender put the cocktail in front of her and said the guy at the end of the bar paid for her drink.

With a discreet glance, she saw it wasn't *him*. "Please return his money. I'll pay for my own drinks." She pushed the fifty toward the bartender.

A guy built like a linebacker made his way from the back of the room through the throng of people and approached her. "Wassup hottie? You're not from around here, are you?" he asked, with the attitude of a Big Man on Campus.

"No Sugar, I'm not. Now, ya'll need to go away and let me be." She found it amusing that he called her an old skank when he left.

Disappointed she hadn't yet seen *him,* she decided she'd give it a little while longer and ordered another drink.

A waitress dressed in a low-cut tank top and skin-tight jeans, called out over the din, "Hey Trey, ready for a refill?"

"No, I'm good, babe."

With casual intent, she turned and locked eyes with *him*, Trey Browning. He leaned against a pillar with a beer mug in his hand. A coy smile from her was all it took. He crossed the room with a confident gait.

Trey walked up to the red-haired woman in the black leather pants. "I like your style, lady. I saw you shoot down that side of beef a minute ago."

"He wasn't my type."

"You gonna do that to me?" He leaned a little closer toward her.

She glanced down to his groin then back to his eyes, "Depends on what you've got to offer, Darlin'."

He whispered close to her ear, "I can give you whatever you like, gorgeous."

"A little full of yourself, aren't you?"

"I'll let you be the judge." His finger touched her neck. "Here, let me fix that for you." He adjusted the collar of her blouse; his hand brushed against her skin. "So, what's your pleasure?"

"I have very specific tastes." She paused. "I'm not sure YOU can satisfy them."

"Lady, whatever you like, I know I can provide."

"Well, Darlin', I'm in the mood for some serious play." She pressed her body against his and softly said, "Got some X?"

"Don't go anywhere without it." He slipped his arm around her waist.

She watched his hungry eyes while she slipped her fingers into her bra and removed several bills. She tucked them into his hand and said, "Darlin' would you like to get us a room?"

She drove behind Trey Browning in her rental car, to the College Pointe Motel. The area was kinetic with music, laughter, and commotion in and out of the rooms. It appeared this motel was where the students went to party—no questions asked. While she waited in her car for him to register, she removed a small makeup bag from the console compartment and double-checked that she had what she'd need.

Trey left the office, passed the breezeway where the vending machines and ice maker were located, walked to the end of the building, opened the door to room 126 and waived at her to come in.

She opened the trunk and grabbed the bottle of vodka she'd purchased earlier and placed it and the cosmetic bag into her Louis Vuitton tote.

She smiled at Trey who waited for her at the door. "I bought this today and I thought I was going to have to drink this all by my lonesome." She put the vodka on the small table next to the window and put the two red plastic cups she brought with her next to the bottle.

Trey walked up behind her, moved her hair away, and kissed her on the neck.

"Ummmm . . . that's nice, but hold on a sec." While she poured the whisky, he continued to nuzzle her neck and reached around to unbutton her blouse. "Slow down, cowboy. We have all night."

He stepped back and reached into his pocket. "Maybe you need a little more inspiration." He opened a small container and dumped four little white pills into his hand. He popped a couple into his mouth and washed them down with a big swig from the liquor bottle. "These are for you." He handed her the rest.

She palmed the pills, acted like she put them into her mouth, and took a sip from the red cup. "Ugh. I can't drink this warm. Be a darlin', run down the hall and bring back some ice."

"You fucking kidding me?" he complained. "Now?"

"Oh, come on. I'll be right here waiting for you," she teased.

On his way out of the room, he grabbed the ice bucket with the plastic liner.

As soon as the door closed behind him, she opened the makeup bag and removed the brown bottle filled with clear liquid. She emptied the contents into his cup. When he returned, she greeted him with a passionate kiss on the lips and handed him his drink. She added the ice to her cup and made a toast. "To fun and surprises."

"I'll drink to that!" He slammed back his tainted drink then poured himself another.

There was a glint of malevolence in his eyes as he reached to unzip her pants.

She slapped away his hand. "Darlin', why don't you take off those nasty ol' clothes and I'll be right back." She positioned her drink on the table and went into the bathroom where she stripped down to her black lace panties, folded her clothes and placed them in a neat pile on the side of the bathtub. She cracked open the door, and from the mirror over the sink outside the bathroom, she saw Trey slip something into her drink, stir it with his finger, and stagger to the bed. *Oh, what a clever boy you are.*

"You ready for me, Darlin'?" she called from the bathroom.

His response was an indistinct slur.

Dressed in only her panties, she walked across the room and retrieved her tote from under the table. She put on latex gloves, removed the zip ties, and climbed on top of his muscular body like a jockey straddles a horse. "Let's play a game."

His lips formed silent words. He struggled to open his eyes.

She crossed his hands over his body as if he was laid out in a coffin, then deftly slipped the zip tie around them and pulled it tight. With little control of his body, he made a feeble attempt to move and was unable to resist the woman half his size. She leaned close to his face and said, "You're going to like this."

She dismounted the incapacitated man, took from the small bag a syringe filled with more of the clear liquid, and climbed back onto his limp body. "Darlin', you look a bit thirsty." She slid the syringe inside his cheek and emptied it into the back of his mouth, then stroked his neck which forced him to swallow.

"That was just a little something to relax you." She leaned over and kissed him on the forehead. "I hear you like Roofies, don't you, Sugar?"

He moaned in response.

She removed the two white pills she had tucked into the waist-band of her panties and slipped them between his parted lips.

"Oh, handsome boy. This is going to be so much fun." She ran her fingers over his chest. "What a beautiful physique you have—so masculine." She slid off his naked body and removed the remainder of the supplies from her tote.

She slipped the larger zip tie around his ankles and secured them. He was unresponsive when she threaded the rope under his bound wrists, raised his arms above his head, and knotted the cord to the spindles of the headboard. She moved to the side of the bed, tucked her hands under his knees, and lifted with all her might. With his ankles bound, his legs plopped wide open like a whore ready to receive her john.

His silk boxers lay on the floor near the bed. She picked them up and stuffed as much of them into his mouth as would fit. When he gagged, she withdrew some of the underwear. "I don't want you to suffocate, Darlin'. But you need to know how the girls you humiliated felt."

Her pace was methodical. First, the shoelace tied tight around his scrotum; then the straight razor. "Trust me. This won't hurt much . . . now." It was over in one quick slash. She dumped the contents of her cup onto the open wound. "Can't have you get an infection now, can we?"

His eyes flew open. He tried to scream and fought against the restraints but sank back into unconsciousness.

She carried the scrotum, testes intact, to the bathroom, stood over the rust stained toilet bowl, released her grip on the 'package,' and flushed.

Systematically, she wiped down anything in the bathroom she might have touched. With a few squares of paper, she wiped the handle of the toilet, flushed again for good measure, and dropped the tissues into the swirling water. She reached for her clothes stacked neat and tidy . . . just how she liked to do everything.

There was a soft groan from Trey. She went to the bedside. He had quieted but tears streamed from the corners of his eyes. She surveyed his crotch. The tourniquet worked. There was little blood, but as an added precaution to ensure minimal bleeding before he was found, she removed the plastic bag filled with ice from the bucket and jammed it between his legs. She cut his arms free from the headboard, lowered his still-bound hands to his abdomen, and tucked the covers gently up under his chin.

"Sleep tight, Darlin'."

With meticulous care, she staged the room. Lights were on, the music on the radio turned up, and she left the door ajar. Good bait for party-goers. It wouldn't take long before he was discovered.

A last look at his unconscious body—she hoped she hadn't given him too much of the drug. Since he hadn't killed, the law of karma didn't call for his death. She only wanted him neutered and humiliated.

It had taken little over an hour to settle the score and balance the scales of justice.

Before she removed the latex gloves, she stuffed the typed note, 'Game Over,' under his pillow, left the room, and with a nonchalant stride across the lot, she climbed in to her car and tossed her bag across the front seat.

Lightning flashed, and thunder clapped. She drove away from the sleazy motel as it began to rain. A couple of miles down the road she removed the long-haired, red wig and shook her own blonde hair loose.

Traffic was light on the interstate with the exception of an occasional big rig. In the distance, an eighteen-wheeler approached on her left. She lowered the window of the car, threw the wig on the road in the path of the truck, and raised the window. The combination of rain, truck tires, and grime should destroy any evidence on the wig. It would be no different than any other roadkill. She'd dispose of the gloves, syringe, and bottle, and clean the straight razor once she got home.

Music from a classical radio station played softly in the background. Ann turned up the volume. The sound of Beethoven's Fifth Symphony filled the car.

CHAPTER NINETEEN

Seated opposite Michael was Ron Browning, an imposing figure who Michael thought had an uncanny resemblance to Elvis Presley in his prime.

"Can I get right to the point, Mr. Vega? My son, Trey was drugged and mutilated. I'm sure you heard about it in the news."

"Mutilated how?" Michael saw the man's face redden and the vein at his temple pulsate.

"Some crazy-ass whore castrated my son like he was a goddamn barnyard animal. He'll never father a child and he'll have to take testosterone for the rest of his life. He's dropped out of school. Attempted suicide. His life is ruined!"

"Mr. Browning, I'm sorry to hear what happened to your son. How can we help you?"

"Listen, I've talked to people. I hear you're a stand-up guy."

Michael grinned. "I guess that depends on which side of the fence you're on."

Browning grinned. "Yeah, I get your point." He leaned back in the chair and seemed more relaxed. He reached inside his jacket pocket and removed a bank envelope. He put it in front of Michael. "I want you to find the bitch who did this."

Michael slid the unopened envelope back toward the man. "Why don't you hold on to this for now, Mr. Browning. I'll need more information from you before I can determine if my agency can help you."

Browning patted the envelope. "Oh, I'm confident you'll take the job."

Michael looked into the cold, dark eyes of a man who was accustomed to buying his way through life. "Hold that confidence, Mr. Browning, until we're done here." Michael had an immediate dislike of the self-absorbed man.

"Fair enough, but there's one more thing, Mr. Vega. My son's been through hell. I don't want him, or the Browning name derided. I want your involvement kept under the radar with the understanding that any information you get, comes directly to me and only to me."

"I'll let you know after I get all the information," Michael told him.

Browning stood and walked to the window to answer the incessant buzz from his phone. He turned to Michael, "Sorry. I need two minutes. It's my office." He stepped out into the waiting area.

Michael's receptionist Sylvie poked her head into the office. "Is there anything I can get for you, boss?"

"No, Sylvie, thanks. Why don't you go to lunch now? I'm all set."

She smiled. "Merci, boss," and closed the door behind her.

Michael doubted if his French-Canadian receptionist would ever lose that French accent. She'd lived in Philadelphia for twenty-five years and worked for S.H.I. long before Connor bought the company. Michael thought it quirky that she still said 'merci.'

Browning returned from his business call, settled in front of Michael and began to talk about his son.

According to him, Trey was perfect. He was a good student and a great athlete. He'd never been in trouble with the law. No steady girlfriend. No alcohol abuse. Drinks a little beer at frat parties. No drug use. Not even a traffic ticket. *A real altar boy!!!*

The boy's father passed two photographs of his son to Michael—one in his football uniform, the other in casual clothes. Trey Browning was tall and well-built like his father. "He's a big boy," Michael said.

Browning smiled proudly. "Yeah, six feet four, two hundred ten pounds." He handed Michael a manila envelope. "Here's the police report along with a composite drawing of the psycho freak, and Trey's hospital records."

"I'll go through these in a minute. But first, Mr. Browning, tell me what your son told you."

"Trey said he went to the Eagle's Nest Bar for a beer with his buddies. Some burned out, red-headed bitch tried to hit on him. He felt sorry for her and didn't want to embarrass her, so he talked to her. She bought him a beer and he didn't want to be rude, so he drank it. The next thing he knew he was tied up in a motel room, people were everywhere, paramedics loaded him into an ambulance.

"His mother and I didn't know how bad he was hurt until we got to the hospital. The damn cops were all over him, badgering him with their questions, acting like they didn't believe him."

"Mr. Browning, do you believe his story?"

"Of course, I believe him! Trey wouldn't lie to me."

While on the force in Tampa, Michael heard a lot of bullshit stories from both vics and perps. His instincts told him there was a lot more to this cock-and-bull account than Ron Browning knew or was telling.

Browning continued, "The fucking cops tried to tell me my son's story doesn't add up, that he doesn't look completely innocent. He was tied up in a motel room and his balls cut off. How is he NOT the victim?"

"Mr. Browning, is it possible he knew his assailant or picked up a prostitute?"

Browning was the epitome of controlled fury. "Listen Mr. Vega, my son's a good-looking kid, always has girls throwing themselves at him. He can't keep them off. He doesn't need to pay for it."

"Does he have a history of problems with any of them?"

"Come on, there's always some lovesick girl who tries to get her hooks into him. He's a football star, or at least he was before——." Browning stood and straightened his jacket. "When you come from a rich family, there's going to be some money-grubbing vulture trying to get pregnant to weasel her way in to our family."

Again, the man's cell rang. Browning took the call and seemed agitated after he finished. "Sorry Mr. Vega, I've gotta leave. Can we finish this over the phone? Goddamn foreman just quit, and I got a whole crew standing around with their thumbs up their asses."

"I believe I have enough of the basics for now, Mr. Browning. I'll be in touch. But if you recall anything else, here's my direct number."

With firm resolve, his client said as he left the office, "My son's a good boy."

Ted Bundy's mother said the same thing.

Michael looked inside the envelope filled with hundred-dollar bills, pushed the pack of money aside and spread the contents of the manila envelope across his desk. He read the police report. The suspect's description at the bottom of the page was that of a white female, approximate age between 30 and 40, 5 feet 3 inches, 120 lbs., red hair, green eyes, no distinguishing scars, tattoos, or birthmarks. Heavy southern accent. It also indicated that Trey described the woman's vehicle as a silver, late model Mustang. The details were all pretty generic.

Michael studied the composite, return it to the envelope with the other documents, and made a note to have Sylvie set up a meeting with Trey's football coach.

CHAPTER TWENTY

The initial background research into the Browning case substantiated some facts that Ron Browning gave about his son. Trey was a starting quarterback and an A/B student in a degree program for business administration.

In a search of public records for any history on Trey Browning, Michael discovered nothing of interest.

Michael studied the paperwork the father had given him. He read the police report like a cop. His gut told him Trey's accounting of the events seemed too rehearsed. Michael knew he'd get more substantive information from Trey's peers.

It was lunchtime when Michael arrived at Vinnie's Cheese Steaks a popular campus eatery for the students. There was a din of conversation in the small space where hungry young people squeezed into every available seat. Michael hadn't realized how famished he was until he smelled peppers and onions cooking on the grill. He walked to the counter and ordered the house special, a cheesesteak 'all the way,' something he had come to love since he moved to Philadelphia. While he waited to pick up his order, Michael introduced himself to the middle-aged man in a white apron that stretched tight over his fat belly. "My name's Michael Vega. I'm doing a story on local college athletes." Michael handed the man a plain business card that showed only his embossed name and phone number.

The corpulent man wiped his hands on his stained apron, took the card and shook Michael's hand. "I'm Vinnie Colombo. I own this joint."

"I'm going to feature the quarterback, Trey Browning," Michael said. "You know him?"

"Yeah, comes in here all the time. Nice kid." Vinnie was eager to boast to Michael how he never missed a game and his nephew, young Vinnie, who is named after him, is a freshman who wants to be a quarterback like Trey. "I take a shitload of steak sandwiches and hoagies over to the locker room on game day. Those guys love my food. We're like one big family."

A line of impatient students backed up behind Michael. Vinnie held up his hand at them, "Hold your horses. This guy's doin' a story about Trey Browning." Vinnie picked up Michael's sandwich, and called over his shoulder, "Hey Joey, take over the counter for me. I'll be right back." Vinnie walked Michael to a booth that was just vacated and bussed and sat across from him. "So, what do you want to know about Trey?"

"How well do you know him?"

"I know he's a hell of a quarterback. Best I've ever seen. The kid deserves the Heisman. Great young man. Not a bad bone in his body." Vinnie lowered his voice. "Damn shame what happened to him though. I don't know if he'll ever play football again."

"How much do you know about what happened?"

Vinnie sat up, "Goddam shame . . . he went to a party at a local motel, got into a fight, and a bunch of punks tied him up and stabbed him pretty bad. He was in the hospital for a long time. A lot of us tried to see him but the father wouldn't allow any visitors."

"Yo, Vinnie!" a voice called from the kitchen.

"Yeah, yeah, yeah. I'm comin'." Vinnie stood, and said, "I'll say this, I hear a lot shit in here. There's talk about a jealous boyfriend, bad debt, even drugs. But I don't believe any of it. Listen, I gotta get back to work. No charge on the sandwich."

"Thanks. That's really nice of you." Michael eyed the overstuffed cheesesteak. "This looks great. Say, if anybody else comes in who you think may want to talk to me, here's a few more of my cards."

On Vinnie's way back to the kitchen, Michael heard him announce that if anybody wanted to talk about Trey, that 'the guy's' sittin' right there.'

Michael was inundated with students excited to talk to him about their football team and their star quarterback. The consensus was that the team had a winning record due to Trey's arm; he never let all the praise go to his head; he always gave credit to the team. Several mentioned that Trey was so generous that he gave money to anyone who asked. They all commented on how big a loss it was for the team to lose him.

Right. Move over Mother Teresa.

One student with dreadlocks that hung below his shoulders, told Michael, "He's a good guy. He can have any prime tail he wants but still 'throws a bone' to the dogs. He says he feels sorry for 'em." The kid laughed, "I've seen some of those bimbos. I couldn't do it."

Michael shook his head, "What a stand-up guy."

The student started to leave. "Guess he finally screwed the wrong girl. I heard a jealous boyfriend and his buddies tried to cut his dick off."

Michael tucked a five-dollar tip under his plate and was ready to head to the Eagle's Nest Bar when a thin, blue-haired young woman approached him. She paused long enough to make eye contact, dropped a folded napkin near his plate then joined a group of students outside who walked toward the campus.

Michael unfolded the napkin and read: *That monster isn't what you think!*

#

The staff at the Eagle's Nest Bar acknowledged to Michael that they knew Trey and remembered that night. The bartender said, "I told the cops all this before. The kid picked up a red-haired dime piece who looked like she was waiting for somebody. He talked to her for a few minutes and they left together."

"A dime piece?" Michael furrowed his brow.

"Sorry dude, you know . . . a dime piece, a piece of ass, a babe. Know what I mean?"

"Yes, I know what a dime piece is."

The bartender insisted Trey didn't appear drunk and he didn't serve him a beer after he hooked up with the redhead. She had a couple of Mojitos, paid with a fifty, and left the change. "Biggest tip I got that week!" He hadn't seen her before or since then.

"Can you take a look at this composite drawing and tell me if this could be the woman you saw with Trey?"

"I don't know, man. Maybe. I paid more attention to her body than her face. Know what I mean?" The man winked.

"What do you know about the College Pointe Motel?"

The bartender laughed. "It's close, it's cheap, and nobody asks questions. Know what I mean?"

"If you think of anything else, I'd appreciate a call." Michael handed the bartender his card.

#

The manager of the College Pointe Motel, like the bartender at The Eagle's Nest, said he'd already talked to the police. He took Michael's business card. "Mister, I run a legitimate business here. It's clean and priced right. Like I told the cops, the guy seemed okay to me when he checked in. He was alone and paid in cash. I didn't know nothin' 'til I heard screamin' and the ambulance showed up."

"What about the security tape?" Michael motioned toward the camera up in the corner of the room behind the desk.

"There was nothin' on it. I didn't know it was broke 'til the cops looked at it. I just got it fixed."

The bells attached to the office door jingled. The manager took the room key from the kid in the Temple University jacket who looked like he had partied all night. The proprietor hung the key on a hook on the wall.

Michael saw the young man climb into a Jeep. "That kid is pretty young. Do you check I.D.'s?"

"I'm done here," the manager said. "You can leave now," and pointed to the door.

Michael announced, "Not for nothing, but you might want to call an exterminator for your clean establishment. There's a big ass cockroach crawling on the wall behind you."

"Get the hell outta here!" Spit sprayed from the man's mouth.

The bells bounced against the glass as Michael closed the door behind him. He walked to his car with a shit-eating grin on his face.

#

Michael retrieved the messages on his cellphone when he returned to his office. Most were in response to the business cards he had left at Vinnie's Cheese Steak's near the campus. The majority of callers didn't give their names but left detailed messages that were not the glowing responses he received at the restaurant.

The one theme that ran through the calls Michael received was that Trey Browning sold ruffies, OxyContin, and any other opioid he could get his hands on. A male caller stated that Trey had his posse beat him up 'pretty bad' because he didn't make his loan payment on time. The caller said he knew of others who had the 'shit kicked out of them' for the same reason.

Another young man said he was a frat brother of Trey's and that on a couple of occasions he heard girls crying in Trey's room but didn't tell anyone because of Trey's infamous temper and his own fear of retribution.

One caller identified herself as the girl from Vinnie's who left him the note on a napkin. He remembered the skinny girl with blue hair who wrote, 'That monster isn't what you think.' Her message indicated that she'd call again at 4:00.

It was 4:45 and Michael was unsure that the girl would call. Fifteen minutes later, a call came in. "Michael Vega."

"I'm the girl who left the note on the napkin." The girl insisted that if Michael went to the police with her story, she would deny she ever said anything.

Michael heard the humiliation and anger in her voice as she recounted the traumatic incident with Trey, how he raped and sodo-mized her in his dorm room, how Trey threatened to kill her if she told anyone, and how he laughed as he shoved her into the empty hallway.

She said she skipped class the next morning and woke to some-one pounding on the door to her room. It was Trey's father, Ron Browning, who told her she couldn't have sex with his son then cry rape. After several threats, Mr. Browning asked her what it would take to make her leave his son alone. She was scared and didn't know how to answer. He handed her an envelope with enough money in it that would more than cover her student loans. She took off a semes-ter and when she returned, she changed her class schedule and avoided Trey at all costs. She never told anybody, but she made it clear to Michael that she was ecstatic that someone finally hurt him bad enough to let him know how it feels to be defenseless.

Finished with the phone call with the anonymous young lady, Michael sat back in his chair, pissed off at the story he heard. Thoughts of the piece-of-shit father, Ron Browning, made Michael's blood boil. What kind of father creates a son like that then defends his behavior.

I was so lucky to have you, Dad.

Michael looked at his wristwatch. He had time to deal with a couple more messages before he met Meg for dinner but was inter-rupted by an incoming call.

"Vega, here."

"Yea, this is Ron Browning. Word got back to me that you were talking to a lot of kids at Vinnie's. I need an update and I want it right away. Meet me at my club tomorrow." He gave Michael the particu-lars and hung up before Michael could respond.

Michael pushed his chair away from the desk. "Oh, sure Mr. Browning, I have nothing on my schedule at noon tomorrow. My only concern is your convenience. Asshole."

The smell of cigar smoke drifted through the office. Whether it was real or imagined, it didn't matter. Michael smiled. He shook off the tension and slid his chair back to the desk.

#

Both men drove up to the country club at the same time. Browning barked at the valet, "Keep my car close. I won't be long."

Once seated in the lounge, Browning got right to the point. "What do you have for me?"

Michael handed him the file.

The scowl on Browning's face while he read the report, spoke volumes.

"Where's the rest of it? I don't see anything in here about the woman I asked you to find." Browning slammed the manila file closed and shoved it toward Michael. "This is bullshit!"

A man at the bar cleared his throat and did not curb his annoyance.

Michael took a deep breath, "What you see is the information that I've found at this—"

Browning lowered his voice. "Trey doesn't deal drugs. I paid you plenty to find the bitch who hurt my son and you hand me rumors."

The muscles in Michael's jaw tightened. "Mr. Browning, before you interrupted me, I started to say that those are unverifiable details which I plan to get to the bottom of." He paused and looked his client square in the eyes. "Have you ever made a payoff to a young woman to avoid, let's call it an assault charge for now, being filed against Trey?"

"Bogus accusations!" Browning raised his voice, "They have nothing to do with what happened to my boy."

Again, the man at the bar cleared his throat and glared.

Michael remained calm. "You can't hold back those details and expect me to do my job."

"Your job, Vega, is to find that woman."

"I know my job and I AM looking for her. But in the course of my inquiries, any 'rumors' I hear about loan sharking, drug deals, rough sex, could be the motive and lead us right to his attacker."

"Loan sharking? Are you out of your fucking mind? What you refer to as rough sex is nothing more than worthless sluts who liked it that way. They should be grateful Trey gave them the time of day, let alone a little attention."

Browning's hands were balled into tight fists. His knuckles, white. "Hold on, Vega. I hired you to find who did this to my kid, not to feed me bullshit."

"Mr. Browning, I'm gathering the pieces, but in order to complete this puzzle, I'm going to have to talk to Trey."

Browning jumped up and grabbed his jacket. "Like hell you are. You're fired!"

CHAPTER TWENTY-ONE

Across the street from Rocco's Tavern, a decaying corner bar on a block of condemned buildings, she waited in the shadows of a boarded-up storefront. The odor of urine and feces, she assumed remnants left by derelicts, assaulted her olfactory senses.

Disguised as a down-and-out teenage boy, Ann was perfect bait for the predator, Elwyn King, who lingered inside the bar.

Her mind reeled with thoughts of destroyed children; the young victims whose aggressors are never convicted; the children neglected to death; innocents denied justice. *How can society be opposed to how I enforce the law? I shouldn't have to hide to balance the scales of justice.*

The disgust she felt when she heard the short sentence the judge ordered did not compare to the anger she experienced when she heard the pedophile was released early from jail after serving only sixty-two-days of his sentence while his fifteen-year-old male victim lay cold in the ground from a self-inflicted gunshot wound.

The media's persistent reporting on the judge and this case revealed enough information about Elwyn King that a blind dog with a head cold could track him.

On his release from jail, King stayed at his mother's home located a few blocks away from where Ann now waited. It had taken several days for the media to lose interest and disperse from around the property. Tonight, he ventured out and had been inside the bar for hours.

The front door to Rocco's opened. A man and a woman stumbled out and staggered on the sidewalk down the deserted avenue. King left the building three-sheets-to-the-wind, tripped on the sidewalk outside the door and caught himself against the brick wall to regain his balance. The exterior lights to the bar went out. King disappeared into the darkness behind the dumpster in the alleyway.

Ann covered her head with the hood of her jacket before she approached King who was pissing like a racehorse. She waited until his stream stopped. "Hey, man," her voice lowered an octave.

The startled drunk eyed the stranger with suspicion.

She stayed in character, "I just scored some good shit. Twenty bucks will get you a great buzz and the best blow job you've ever had."

He hesitated and gave her an enigmatic look. "Sure kid . . . got y'self ah deal." He handed her a couple of crumpled bills, popped the pills into his mouth, and swallowed. King shuffled back into the privacy behind the dumpster.

The man unzipped his pants, leaned against the wall, and closed his eyes. As drunk as he was, the effect of the drug hit him fast. King's soft member did not respond to her touch. He didn't seem to notice or care that the person holding his dick wore surgical gloves.

He moaned, "Whad'ya . . . gimmeee?" and slid down the wall. He rolled to the pavement and lay flat on his back in the puddle of his own piss.

A quick glance at the man's face made it clear that he was zonked. *Told you it was good shit.* She held the pink stun gun to King's temple, watched the electricity arc against his head, and waited until his body stopped convulsing. Confident he was incapacitated, she used the straight razor and sliced through King's exposed manhood. She put the oozing penis and the instrument into a plastic sandwich bag, stepped over the massive pool of blood flowing from King, and left a typed note, 'A short sentence,' amid the trash.

Seized by panic when she heard the loud bang of the heavy metal backdoor of the bar, she took off running.

"Hey, you!" a man yelled. "That's right. Keep runnin' punk and don't come back."

Ann turned the corner and heard the man shriek. *Guess he found*

King. She returned to the vacant building where she had stashed her backpack under newspaper in the corner of the storefront earlier that evening.

Hidden in the darkness of the entryway, she stripped off the gloves, blood spattered sweatpants, and hoodie to reveal clean running clothes she wore beneath. She reached inside the bag and removed a ball cap and a bottle of water. She rinsed her face and hands and stuffed the soiled clothes along with the gloves, water bottle, and the plastic bag containing the straight razor and trophy, into the backpack.

The sound of police sirens preceded the procession of emergency vehicles. They headed in the direction of Rocco's.

Ann retreated into the shadows of the storefront and waited for them to pass. Confident she was in the clear, she put her hair into a ponytail, slung the backpack over her shoulder, stayed close to the buildings, and walked to her car that she had left a couple of blocks away.

A news van, headed toward the commotion at Rocco's, sped passed her car as she approached the ramp of the freeway.

In a secluded spot in her condo building's underground garage out of view of the security cameras, Ann removed the sheet of painter's plastic that she used to cover the floor and front seat of her car. *No trace evidence left behind.*

She wadded the plastic into a ball and threw it into the commercial dumpster. It was concealed in plain sight among the array of trash bags, boxes, and refuse to be picked up by city workers Monday morning.

The adrenaline rush had left her and now she was exhausted. Ann was desperate for a hot shower and sleep but first she had to wash the clothes and the bag in gallons of bleach. Those items would be put in plastic grocery bags in the morning and thrown into various dumpsters. The water bottle was stuffed in the trash compactor and the plastic bag that contained the trophy and the razor was tossed in the freezer.

"Karma, Elwyn King. Karma."

CHAPTER TWENTY-TWO

Judge Franklin Carroll was a creature of habit which made it easy for Ann to monitor his routine. On this pleasant Autumn day, she waited for him on his usual bench where he was delighted to find her. They spoke about life, politics, and books. The thought crossed her mind, if the circumstances were different that perhaps they could have been friends.

There was little variation to his daily schedule and generally he left his home at six-fifteen p.m. for his evening meal. Tuesday was his day for dinner at the local chop house. While he dined at the restaurant, she went to his apartment on the pretext of delivering a book that they had discussed. A brilliant excuse for being seen in his building. She would kill two birds with one stone. It would give her the perfect opportunity to scrutinize the location of cameras and locate the emergency exits, if needed.

She was pleased to discover how little security there was in the exclusive luxury tower. The only cameras that she would have to be concerned with were those in the lobby.

Pleased with her reconnaissance of the judge's building, Ann walked nonchalantly home, poured herself a glass of wine, and reconfirmed her reservations at Resorts Hotel & Casino in Atlantic City.

#

Outside the chop house, Judge Carroll paused in the crisp, clear evening air to light his cigar. He crossed the street and walked through the park across from his apartment. The lighted square was alive with activity. An elderly man sat on a bench and played a violin; his open instrument case lay on the ground in front of him. A hand-written note on cardboard, Thank You and God Bless, was propped up against the tattered red velvet lining. The judge stopped in front of the old man, nodded, and added loose change from his pockets to the smattering of coins and dollar bills that lay inside the case. An energetic Pitbull puppy fought against its leash while a teenage girl struggled to gain control of the dog. A young couple stopped to buy hot soft pretzels from a vendor.

The judge crossed the street and walked up to the door of the ornate old building where he lived. Before he entered, he snuffed out his cigar and waited in the empty lobby for the elevator. He stepped into the camera-less lift. The heavy doors closed behind him.

#

She dressed while she waited for the activities in the park to end. It would take a while for the people to disperse. She stood in front of the mirror and admired her transformation into what appeared to be a young man. With bound breasts and no makeup, all she'd have to do is walk like a guy.

The canvas grocery sack with the plastic bag from the freezer was rolled up and tucked under Ann's arm before she left her condo.

The back stairs of her building provided the ideal exit onto the street without being noticed by any of her curious neighbors. She pulled her hair up under her baseball cap and added horn-rimmed glasses before she left the security of the stairwell.

The boyish figure in the red ball cap kept a steady pace toward the judge's building, taking a short-cut through the now quiet square.

Sure to keep her head down to avoid being identified, she walked through the lobby of his building. Inside the elevator, Ann removed the glasses and baseball cap, and shook her thick blonde hair loose. The heavy brass doors opened to an empty hall. She stopped at the trash door where she stomped on the glasses and thrust them inside the shoot. Broken glasses in the trash would not draw anyone's attention. She shoved the red hat in the sack and would leave it on a bench on the boardwalk when she got to Atlantic City. Someone would pick it up.

Ann took a tube of lipstick from her pocket, slid the glossy red color over her lips, and fluffed her hair. She knocked on Judge Carroll's door and saw the cover over the peephole, open. "Franklin is your invitation to stop by for a drink still valid?"

He opened the door wide. "What a lovely surprise. Entre vous." He bowed and motioned for her to enter.

CHAPTER TWENTY-THREE

The repugnant smell of garlic and cabbage accosted Ann's senses when she stepped off the elevator. *Mrs. Bolinski is cooking again.* How she despised her obnoxious, nosey neighbor. Ann hurried past the gossip's front door which opened right on cue.

"Oh, hello, Ms. Paxton." The seventy-ish woman who wore a seersucker house dress, sneakers and white ankle socks, greeted her with enthusiasm.

Damn. "Hello, Mrs. Bolinski," Ann said, as she continued toward her apartment wheeling her carryon bag behind her.

The woman called out to her, "How was your trip?"

"It was relaxing. I went to Atlantic City . . . for some peace and quiet."

"Oh, how nice." The woman went on, "Did you hear what happened to the judge who lived in the building across the square? There was so much commotion—"

Ann acted like she didn't hear the woman, picked up the papers that had been delivered while she was gone, and opened the door to her apartment. It was almost closed behind her when she heard the ping of the elevator door as it opened. Mrs. Boliniski had cornered someone else. "Hello, Mr. Rovner. Did you hear what happened to . . ."

Relaxed on the sofa with a glass of wine, Ann propped up her feet on the ottoman, and unfolded a newspaper.

The headline on the front page read:

Controversial Judge Found Dead in His Home

100

Judge Franklin Carroll, 72, was found dead of an apparent suicide, in his downtown apartment by his housekeeper when she arrived for work.

Judge Carroll sat on the bench in the Philadelphia courts for more than twenty years. In 1999, he turned down a request to run for the State Senate.

Evidence was discovered with Judge Carroll's body that connects him to the recent murder of Elwyn King whose mutilated corpse was found last week in an alley in the Kensington area of Philadelphia.

Judge Carroll was involved in a previous controversy which caused a public outcry for him to be removed from the bench. His reputation as a stern but fair jurist was tainted by his egregious light sentence of Elwyn King who was accused of the rape of a fifteen-year-old boy. Elwyn King was released this month after serving sixty-two days of his sentence.

During sentencing, Judge Carroll said that the boy, Lawrence Lee, was big for his age and looked much older than fifteen. The judge stated that King believed the young man was over the age of eighteen and that the sex was consensual.

The victim, Lee, who accused King of rape, shot himself in the chest when he returned home from the trial. He died the next day . . .

Ann read the article several times, cut it from the paper and wrote 'a JUST sentence' across the column, put it an envelope marked 'Lawrence Lee,' and added it to her 'Dead' file that she kept in the cabinet.

She poured another glass of wine, sat on the sofa, and pondered how much did her actions matter in the scheme of life. Regardless, she would continue her mission.

The sauvignon blanc exacerbated her hunger. Rather than cook, she opted to walk to the café for dinner.

The instant she stepped into the hallway, Ann was accosted by Mrs. Bolinski and was held captive at the elevator by the old windbag.

"Ms. Paxton, how exciting to speak to you twice in one day. You won't believe what I just heard." She held her hand up. "This is the God's honest truth. Leroy, our doorman, knows Judge Carroll's housekeeper. She told Leroy the judge slashed his wrists. There was blood everywhere."

Ann pushed the call button. "I just read the article about the poor judge's suicide, Mrs. Bolinski. I have to run. I'm meeting someone for dinner." The elevator doors opened but before Ann could enter, Mrs. Bolinski tugged on Ann's sleeve.

"Wait, wait, there's more." The old gossip sounded like a hyped-up television commercial pitchman.

The doors of the empty elevator closed in front of Ann.

Mrs. Bolinski leaned closer. "When his housekeeper found him, he had a razor in one hand," she whispered, "and a cut-off penis in the other." She paused long enough to take a breath. "Can you imagine . . . a penis!"

"Mrs. Bolinski, that rumor is too gruesome for me to think about." Ann pressed the call button with increased urgency. This time when the elevator doors opened, Ann put her hand inside to prevent them from closing. "As I said, I'm on my way to dinner although with the details you shared with me, I believe I've lost my appetite."

Ann left an open-mouthed Mrs. Bolinski alone in the hall.

CHAPTER TWENTY-FOUR

Jane Mara stood in front of the gilded mirror in her dressing room and assessed her outfit. The rich darkness of the black silk dress complimented the iridescence of her pearls, the strand Gary gave her to wear on their wedding day. It was the perfect outfit to wear for their anniversary dinner. Gary liked her in a simple and classic style. It was a far cry from the tattered clothes she wore in the broken-down trailer in Ohio so many years ago.

One last check of her makeup; she was satisfied Gary would approve. She smoothed a stray strand of hair behind her ear and wondered, as she had since she was a child, who she resembled. Was it her mother? Did she too have brown eyes, straight black hair, and high cheek bones? Was it her father who gave her the light complexion? Did he know he had a child? Would her curiosity about her parents ever end?

The distinctive rev of his Porsche in the driveway signaled Gary's arrival. Jane hurried so as not to keep him waiting, one of his pet peeves. She was excited to give him the gold studs and cufflinks he had written down on his wish list and hoped Gary had gotten her the bracelet she wanted after all of her hints.

Jane rushed down the stairs and out the front door. Gary unexpectedly held open the passenger door for her, a courtesy he stopped some time ago.

"Well, aren't you gorgeous," Gary smiled.

"And you are as handsome as ever." Jane kissed him on the cheek. "Gary, is that a new jacket?"

"Yes, it is. I bought it to keep at the hospital in case I have an unexpected meeting after work and I don't have enough time to come home and change."

A wave of uncertainty washed over her. She fought hard to keep the old insecurities at bay. "I understand," she tried to sound unaffected. She slid into the car, and said with confidence, "I have a pleasant change of plans for us, Gary. We'll need to head to center city. I've changed our dinner reservations to Scarpetta."

"What? I thought we were going to dinner at Mama DiNardo's." Gary sounded more annoyed than pleased. He shut the door and got in behind the wheel. "Jane, you know I don't like to be blindsided."

"Please do this for me. This is a special occasion, Gary, and Scarpetta is where you proposed."

"I know where I proposed, Jane." Gary downshifted, made the turn toward the restaurant, and accelerated faster than was necessary.

Jane raised her voice in competition with the noise of the engine, "Gary don't be upset with me. I thought . . ."

Gary didn't respond and was quiet the remainder of the ride.

#

"Good evening, Ms. Paxton." The maître d' escorted Ann to her reserved table. "How nice to see you," he said.

"Thank you, Kurtz."

A commotion at the entrance of the restaurant elicited Ann's attention. Her obnoxious neighbor, Mrs. Bolinski, argued with the hostess. "No, I don't want to sit at a table. I want a booth! I'll wait for Kurtz. He knows where I like to sit." Poor Mr. Bolinski stood silent as usual, eyes averted to the floor.

"Kurtz," Ann whispered to the maître d', "please tell me you won't seat them anywhere near me."

"I understand, Ms. Paxton." He hurried to the front of the restaurant. "Good evening, Mr. and Mrs. Bolinski. Right this way."

Ann turned away from the scene so as not to be recognized by Mrs. Bolinski. Certain they had been seated across the room, Ann turned back to see the George Clooney look-alike enter with an attractive woman. *Not the usual one.* The couple was seated across the room; the woman faced in Ann's direction. There was something about her that Ann found difficult to ignore. She forced herself to turn away. Her thoughts turned to the judge and Elwin King. It was a toss-up as to who was worse, the pedophile or the complicit judge. Regardless, the hand of karma resolved the issue.

#

The waiter brought a bucket of ice and the bottle of champagne that Jane had preordered. He filled their glasses, replace the bottle in the ice bucket, wished them a happy anniversary and left.

"How thoughtful, Jane." Gary picked up his glass. "To you, sweetheart. Happy anniversary."

"And, happy anniversary to you." Jane handed him the box she put in her purse before she left the house. She waited with excited anticipation as Gary unwrapped his gift.

"Wow, Jane. You actually read my wish list." He kissed her cheek. "They're really nice but I feel so bad. I should have mentioned that I had a jeweler design a tuxedo set for me that I picked up the other day. I'm sorry. I should have scratched it off my list. But I'm sure you can return these."

Jane suppressed the hurt. She forced a smile and reached into the gift bag he handed her. He had given her a bottle of perfume, a fragrance she didn't like. The discount drugstore price tag was left on the bottle. It was obvious that her gift was a last-minute thought. Jane dropped the bottle back into the bag and excused herself from the table.

#

Mrs. Bolinski's distinctive cackle resounded through the dining room. Her animated laugh was to Ann like fingernails scraping across a blackboard. Other diners turned in the direction of the outburst. The beautiful dark-haired woman seemed oblivious to the commotion. Ann fixated on her, watched her leave the table and head toward the Ladies' Lounge.

The irresistible urge to go to her was like an intense magnetic pull which Ann couldn't resist.

#

Jane stood at the sink, fixed her makeup, and smoothed her hair. In the reflection of the mirror, she saw a woman who stood behind her locked in a stare. Embarrassed, Jane turned to leave.

"Janie, is that you?"

Jane froze, a look of bewilderment on her face. "Annie? Oh my God!" she screamed. Flabbergasted, Jane put her hand to her mouth. "Annie, is it really you?"

They stood face to face astounded, then reached out to one another and embraced as if they would never let go. Ann fought hard to hold back tears while Jane sobbed.

The women asked the other simultaneously, "What are you doing here?" The mutual questions and answers shot back and forth like a tennis match. They were so caught up in their conversation, they paid little attention to the women who entered the powder room and gave them curious looks.

"I've missed you so much," Jane declared. "I searched and searched for you." She hugged Ann like a child. "I thought I'd never see you again. I've told Gary about you—oh my gosh, Gary! You've got to come and meet my husband." Jane took Ann by the hand and led her to where Gary waited for her return.

He stood when he saw his wife and another woman approach. "Jane, are you okay? You were gone so long I was concerned about you."

"Oh Gary, the most amazing miracle has happened." Jane's arm was wrapped around Ann's waist. "This is my sister Annie!"

106

Ann extended her hand to the familiar, handsome man, whom she learned was married to her foster-sister. "Please call me, Ann." Sure that Jane couldn't see her face, Ann looked deep into his eyes with a deadpan regard. "It's nice to meet you," she said.

"Ann, it's rare that I forget a face. Have we met?"

"It's possible. I live in the towers next door and usually dine here on Thursdays. I must have seen you here." She waited, amused by his discomfort.

"That's doubtful." Gary stammered, "I haven't eaten here in years."

Jane slid across the booth and motioned for Ann to sit next to her. "Ann, we have so much catching up to do." They talked about Florence and how she would dress them in matching sister dresses, and the homemade cookies she would have ready for them after school.

"Jane, I've never forgotten your infectious giggles as I read to you. You couldn't understand why Scarlett O'Hara was told to eat before she went to a barbecue."

"Oh my gosh, I still have that book. I keep it in the drawer next to my bed. It's kind of beat up, but I'd never get rid of it."

The waiter approached with their escargot and said to Gary, "Sir, shall I set another place?"

"By all means, Ann," Gary offered, "you're welcome to join us for our anniversary dinner." The emphasis on 'our.'

Jane shot Gary an incredulous look, mortified at his tactlessness; her cheeks flushed.

"That's very sweet of you, Gary," Ann said, "but I wouldn't think of intruding on your romantic evening, besides, I_have someone waiting for me at the theater and I won't be able to reach them by phone to cancel. Jane, we have plenty of time for reminiscing." Ann hugged Jane goodbye, and said, "I can't wait to talk to you. Here's my number, please call me in the morning."

Jane, with her glare still on Gary, said, "I'm so disappointed." She took Ann's hand in hers. "Well, if you can't join us now, then I insist you come to our home for dinner tomorrow. I won't take no for an answer." She texted their information to Ann. "We'll see you at six p.m."

It would have been awkward for Ann to sit alone and finish her meal after Gary's insincere invitation to join them. She stopped at the maître d' station, slipped Kurtz cash and asked him to have her dinner delivered to her condo upstairs.

#

The earlier disappointment in their anniversary celebration forgotten, Jane's conversation throughout the remainder of the meal was effervescent. She rambled on telling stories about growing up with Ann. It wasn't until Jane mentioned that Ann was clairvoyant that Gary interjected.

"Do you really expect me to buy that crazy nonsense?" His barrage of sarcastic comments about the existence of any kind of paranormal ability, offended Jane. While she tried to explain to him some of the events she witnessed with Ann when they were children, he smirked and said, "I know that children brought up in foster care can be a little emotionally unstable. You know, Jane, there's very little difference between psychic and psychotic."

Jane squared her shoulders, and said, "The difference is that psychotics say things that never happen, and a true psychic can predict future events."

Gary laughed out loud, "Yeah, right Jane."

"Just this once, can you please not give me that 'holier than thou' look, Gary?"

"I have a medical background, Jane. You're never going to convince me, but if it makes you happy, I'll listen."

"Gary, you know I don't exaggerate. I was with Ann at a 4th of July picnic when she told me that our foster-mother's father was going to die in a car crash around Christmas. He was killed by a drunk driver on New Year's Eve. Then there was the time we were at vacation bible school when Ann told our classmates that our church would burn down. Later that summer there was a terrible storm and the building was struck by lightning and destroyed.

"Gary, will you stop rolling your eyes and just listen? Before the NASA space shuttle Challenger was scheduled to launch in 1986, Ann said she saw that something bad was going to happen to the teacher on board. I remember when she told the Vice Principal about it. He laughed and told her not to worry, that NASA had everything under control. Two days later, we were all in assembly and saw the explosion."

"Enough Jane . . . I've heard all I can stomach. Do me a favor, please don't ever tell these stories to anybody else. It makes you look asinine and as your husband, how do you think that bodes for me?"

A tear rolled down her cheek. Jane lowered her head. "I want to go home."

"I'm sorry our anniversary dinner was spoiled, Jane. The evening didn't work out like I had hoped. Next week I'll take you to Mama DiNardo's like I originally planned, and we'll have a do-over. Will it make you happy if I get you that bracelet you wanted?"

She didn't answer.

CHAPTER TWENTY-FIVE

With the exception of the miniature replica of their home for a mailbox Ann passed on her way in, she admired the details of the property. Her sister's exquisite red brick Georgian house and artful gardens could have made the cover of House Beautiful Magazine. Ann left her car in the circular driveway and rang the doorbell at six p.m. sharp.

"Come in, come in," Jane urged. She hugged Ann then guided her through the marble entryway and into the living room.

Ann took in the beauty of the antique-filled parlor with its tasteful deep blue and cream-colored appointments and handed Jane a bottle of wine. "Your home is gorgeous, Jane. This is a far cry from Don and Florence's house in Ohio."

"Thank you. It's been a long road." Jane put the bottle of wine on the wet bar. "Gary will be a little late. Make yourself comfortable, I'll be right back."

Jane returned from the kitchen with a chilled bottle of white wine and hors d'oeuvres, dates stuffed with goat cheese, and curried shrimp. The sisters reminisced while they leafed through a photo album that Jane had readied in anticipation of Ann's arrival. There was a picture of Jane when she graduated nursing school, but most were of Gary and Jane's wedding and their honeymoon in Tahiti.

Jane explained that her 'incredible and happy life' hadn't begun until she met Gary. "Ann, he's brilliant and compassionate. His patients adore him and so do I. I can't wait until you get to know him better."

"And, I look forward to it, as well." Ann pointed to one of the pictures. "Jane, you made a beautiful bride. You know, I don't have many photos," Ann said, "but I do have one that I treasure. Do you remember

110

when we had our picture taken in those matching blue dotted Swiss dresses?" Jane didn't answer. "Don't you remember?"

Jane's mood was pensive.

"I remember," Jane replied in a quiet voice. "I kept that dress for years, but it got lost while I lived in Millerstown."

"I'll have a copy of the photo made for you if you'd like."

The atmosphere in the room changed.

Jane blurted out, "Where did you go? Why didn't you come to see me? Did you ever think about me?"

"Jane, I—,"

"Didn't you care what happened to me?" Jane's voice quivered like a child's.

"Of course, I thought about you, but I assumed you'd be okay. Don and Florence loved you and were good to you." Ann reached for her hand. "Jane, I did call the house on your eighteenth birthday, but Florence said you had met a nice young man and gotten engaged and that you had recently moved to Millerstown. She said you hadn't contacted them after that and it was like you vanished off the face of the earth. She was a little worried, and hurt, but believed you were ashamed of your past and wanted to start a new life."

"That wasn't my intention. I guess we all assumed things that weren't accurate." Jane checked the time. "I have to admit I'm glad Gary's a little late. It gives us more time to talk. But enough about me, please Ann, tell me about you. Where did you go? What did you do?"

"Honestly Jane, there's not much to tell; nothing out of the ordinary. The first few years after I left home, my life was a little upside down. I waitressed at a truck stop and eventually married a trucker and moved to Oregon. That relationship was short-lived. By then, my life had become a string of . . . well . . . let's close the door on the past and focus on our future. Jane, we have so many new memories to make." Ann popped a stuffed date into her mouth. "Um, scrumptious."

It was clear the subject of Ann's past was closed, and Jane didn't press the issue.

A little before nine p.m. Gary rushed in still dressed in dark purple scrubs. He apologized for being late and gave Jane a peck on the cheek. "The moon's full. All the crazies end up in the ER. Thanks for holding dinner. Let me run up and shower. I'll be right down."

Dinner conversation was pleasant. Gary was full of compliments about the great cook that Jane had become since they were first married. He actually had to 'send her to a culinary school or starve to death.' He teased, "But she refuses to cook my favorite food."

"I've told you a hundred times, Gary, that the smell of bacon makes me ill," Jane said.

Ann said to Jane, "May I have another serving of that delicious roast? Gary's right, you are a superb cook." Ann took another bite of food.

Gary refilled the wine glasses and said, "Jane mentioned you're a clairvoyant consultant. How does that work?" he asked with a note of condescension. "How and when did you learn to do that?"

Ann chewed with deliberate slowness, patted the corners of her mouth with her napkin, took a drink of her wine, then answered him in a flat tone. "What I have is something you can't learn. I was born with what is known as a sixth sense."

"A sixth sense? Well, that's a debatable point," he smirked. "As a physician, I'm only aware of five senses."

"It's complicated, Gary. Not everyone can understand. It's a lengthy subject. Let's save this discussion for another time."

The muscles in Gary's jaw tightened. He persisted, "After what Jane has told me about your background, I'm quite interested, even if I don't believe in psychics."

"Gary, your skepticism is accepted," Ann stated. "Jane, tell me how you came to collect such extraordinary antiques?"

"It started on our first trip to New York. I saw a Chippendale chair—,"

"So, Ann," Gary interrupted, "would you be considered a fortune teller?"

"Gary!" Jane exclaimed.

"No, I would not." Ann pushed away her plate.

112

"Gary, can you help me clear the dishes so I can serve dessert?" Jane prodded.

He glowered at Jane, "Don't try to change the subject. I'm asking Ann for a specific reason. Rumors are rampant on the golf course at our club about the suspicious circumstances surrounding the recent suicide of one of our board members. I read in the paper that fortune tellers are coming out of the woodwork with offers to help the police solve the mystery. Ann, I thought you might be one of them."

"No, I'm not, and I don't work with the police." There was an unmistakable edge in Ann's voice.

Gary went on. "The old guy was quite a gentleman, and well known. As a matter of fact, he lived in your neighborhood, Ann. Maybe you knew him . . . Judge Franklin Carroll."

"Honestly, I had never heard of him until I read about his horrible suicide in the paper."

"That remark calls for a change of subject," Jane said. "I'm going to bring in dessert."

Ann addressed Gary without expression. "Jane shared with me your wedding album. You were a beautiful couple. My sister told me how she adores you. She's lucky to have such a loyal and devoted husband."

Again, the muscles in Gary's jaw tensed. "In truth, I'm the lucky one." He returned the same expressionless gaze to Ann.

"Aw, Gary. That's so sweet," Jane said as she walked in and set a tray of pastry in front of him. "I hope you're not saying that because I made one of your favorite desserts."

"No, I'm not just saying that. I couldn't have a better wife."

For the remainder of the evening, conversation was light and ended on a high note for the sisters to meet for lunch at the end of the week.

As Ann drove away she saw Gary and Jane standing in the open doorway, arm in arm.

Do you really think you're fooling me, Gary?

CHAPTER TWENTY-SIX

Ann left the photo shop with a copy of the picture she promised Jane. On her walk back to her office, the earlier heavy mist had turned to a steady rain. She opened her umbrella and quickened her step. As she approached the office building, a homeless man had stopped for refuge, his back pressed against the brick wall to avoid the cold soaking rain, a plastic trash bag held in his tight grip. She assumed the bag was filled with his worldly goods. Ann stopped under the awning at the entrance of her building, handed him her umbrella, a twenty-dollar bill, and continued into the lobby.

In her office, Ann removed the package from her tote, the photograph she had duplicated and framed and positioned it next to the clock on her desk. The fond memory the picture evoked, warmed Ann.

Her thoughts drifted to her evening with Jane and Gary. The unpleasantness of her conversation with him at dinner was outweighed by her joy of reuniting with Jane.

A light tap on the door signaled that Beth Owen was there for her reading.

The pretty young dental assistant appeared more distraught than usual. She sat across from Ann and fidgeted with the Malachite worry stone Ann had given her on her first visit. This would be her third reading in as many months.

Beth's thirty-year-old boyfriend, Eric Prins, worked as a lineman for the power company. He moved in with her a few weeks after they started dating. They lived together for less than a year.

At the start of their relationship, Eric was thoughtful, funny, and attentive, but their storybook romance ended like a dark fairytale.

His unannounced romantic visits to her office 'just to say hello' started as occasional sweet gestures but soon became excessive intrusions. At her boss' insistence, Beth asked Eric not to come by her work anymore. Angered, Eric agreed but began calling her cellphone throughout the day. At first, she thought his calls were because he loved her so much. When she was too busy to speak with him, she would find him after work on his motorcycle waiting for her.

Eric accused her of 'screwing' the dentist and was adamant that she quit her job and insisted that he could take care of her. She assured Eric that she loved only him but that she would not leave her job. He swore 'she wouldn't have a job to go to' if she didn't quit.

Over that weekend, a blaze broke out at the dental office. The fire marshal declared the cause an electrical system failure.

Beth disregarded the coincidence and refused to consider Eric had anything to do with the fire.

Eric's obsessive jealousy turned to enraged anger when he overheard Beth's sympathetic phone conversation with her boss about the damage. Eric ripped the handset away from her and threw it against the wall. It was then that Beth found the recording device in the broken phone.

Beth ordered Eric to leave immediately. She turned a deaf ear to his pleas to forgive him and reconsider. He shouted from the front lawn that she would have to take him back or he'd make sure nobody else would ever want her.

After his eviction, her tires were slashed, the wires outside of her house were cut from the box, and she discovered her Orange Tabby, dead, it's head crushed under a cinder block in the middle of the driveway.

She went to the police and did everything they suggested which included changing the locks and installing a security system. There was nothing more the police could do without proof that it was Eric who was behind these incidents.

Ann's tone was low and firm, "Beth, I warned you at your first session not to get involved with him but if you let him into your life he wouldn't be there long. I said that while he was there he would be a destructive force that would destroy everything in his path. You do remember, don't you?"

Beth lowered her head.

Ann continued, "Of course, Eric is responsible for all of those events, including the cat, and he won't be caught."

"I remember what you said, but I thought I could change him."

"Beth, I told you from the start that he was no good and that this relationship would end badly."

"I know I made a mistake, Ann. How can I get him out of my life?"

"Beth, don't expect me to correct your mistakes after I warned you how to avoid them." Ann sighed, "Let it go. Karma will take care of Eric."

#

It had been a long week of whining clients with mundane problems. Relieved the interminable week was behind her, Ann looked forward to meeting Jane for lunch. She got into her car, turned on the seat warmer, and the radio.

". . . a spokesman for the DOT, tells us to expect traffic backups of two hours or more." The announcer continued, "What we know at this time is a fatal accident involving a motorcyclist has shut down I-95 northbound by the Philadelphia International Airport. It appears the victim was hit by a cinder block thrown from an overpass. He was a thirty-year-old employee of the Philadelphia Power Company. His name has not been released pending notification of next of kin."

Ann said, "Karma Eric, karma."

CHAPTER TWENTY-SEVEN

The dark gray sky threatened snow. At the front door, Michael kissed Meg goodbye and reminded her to be careful on her drive home. This was the first time she had stayed over at his apartment. He never believed he could feel so in love again. It felt so natural to wake up with her beside him in his bed.

No matter what time Michael got to his office, Sylvie always had a hot cup of coffee and the morning newspaper waiting for him. He had long since given up trying to figure out how she knew when he'd show up, but somehow, she did. He reached for his cup, scanned the front page of the paper, and noticed the caption, 'Browning Construction Settles Multi-Million Dollar Lawsuit.' The article mentioned that homeowners were awarded funds for the damage caused by the Chinese drywall that Browning's company had used when constructing the Cove Lane neighborhood in Runnemede, New Jersey. Browning's defense was that his company did nothing wrong and that the blame should fall on the subcontractors he hired.

"It's not your fault? Or you couldn't find someone to buy-off this time, Browning?" Michael smiled, turned the page and saw that the upcoming International Law Enforcement Symposium would be held in the Philadelphia Convention Center. He hadn't been to a police convention since he and Steve DeMarcou attended the one in Las Vegas. He felt bad he hadn't spoken to Steve since Connor died. There was no reason why other than Michael's life had become so busy with work that time had gotten away from him. He picked up the phone and dialed Steve's number in Florida.

#

Law enforcement officers from around the world walked up and down the aisles of the convention center. Displayed on the main floor were the most current technological advances in firearms and protective gear along with reconnaissance equipment and specialized electronic devices. Michael was most interested in the latter. He stopped at a demonstration on the newest riot control and disaster survival equipment.

Michael and Steve were supposed to meet in front of the Israelis' booth. Steve was late, and Michael was about to text his buddy when he caught sight of him. "Hey man, don't I know you?" The two men greeted each other as only old friends can do. "Steve, it's great to see you, and how's that gorgeous wife of yours?"

"Allison's great. You'll see for yourself at dinner tonight."

Their reunion was interrupted by the crackle of a microphone. The speaker identified himself as a former member of the Mossad. The guys listened as the Israeli discussed new lightweight weapons for law enforcement. When the presentation finished, the two friends ambled along the aisles and stopped on occasion to hear a salesman hawk his wares. As they walked around, they caught up on family news. Michael appreciated the fact that Steve didn't bring up the topic of his ex-wife, Teresa. Instead, he asked about the new woman in Michael's life.

"You look good, buddy," Steve said. "Life must be treating you right."

"To be honest, I've got a few bumps and bruises I never got as a cop. You guys have it easy with that badge to protect you." Michael joked, "Down here in the gutter is where the real shit happens." The expression on Steve's face made Michael laugh. "If you want another career after you retire—"

"No thanks. Allison likes me just the way I am . . . intact."

It was late afternoon when the two friends said goodbye. Michael said he and Meg would pick up Steve and Allison at their hotel and take them to dinner at the gourmet Italian restaurant on Ritten-house Square.

#

The lady who walked into Ann's office was a big woman, from her hair to her derriere. She wore large hoop earrings, floral print spandex capris and a matching pullover that accentuated her muffin top. Her energy was like a lot of Ann's clients, hyper and stressed. The woman said her husband came home after work four months ago, handed her an envelope filled with cash, and told her he had to go away for a while but that he'd be in touch with her. She hadn't heard from him since he left that day.

She told Ann he was very generous and often brought her gifts from work like small appliances and household items. Once, he gave her three iPads. She explained that it was normal for him and the other dock workers to help themselves to a little excess cargo that nobody would miss. "He did mention he thought he and buddies were being spied on, but I can't believe he'd leave because of that." She wanted to know when he was coming home.

"My friend who recommended you, said I should show you this photograph of my husband—she said you might be able to tell me where he's at. It's a pretty recent picture. That's him," she pointed to the man who stood next to a pickup truck. "He was so happy there. That was the day he brought his truck home from the paint shop." The woman puffed, "You know, he was at a bar with his buddies having a few beers and drew that design on a napkin and had it painted on his truck. He's so talented and the biggest Eagles fan."

"My goodness, that's certainly original," Ann commented. *A green flying eagle in Philadelphia.* Ann's eyes were intent on the photograph. She knew the man was dead. "Your husband isn't coming home. He's—"

"He's cheating again, isn't he?" The animated lady, "I knew it! I just knew it." She huffed, "That piece of scum gave me fifty grand

and he thought that would buy me off? Was it that blonde barmaid again?" She didn't wait for an answer and continued her diatribe. "I'll tell you what, I'm gonna take him for every cent he's got, sell the house and that goddamn boat of his. When he comes back begging for me, I'll be gone."

Ann sat back and allowed the woman to rant and rant she did, about the brunette, the redhead, their neighbor, and the dealer in Atlantic City.

The worked-up woman finished, her face was beet-red and dripped with perspiration. She stood to leave and thanked Ann for her help. "Ms. Paxton, you're absolutely amazing. Now I know what I have to do, and I'll stop worrying about that good-for-nothing husband of mine." She handed Ann her fee and said, "Just like my friend said, you're worth every penny." She left an amused Ann seated at her desk.

Ann chuckled to herself. It was the first time she'd ever witnessed a 'selfie' reading.

It had been a bizarre week for Ann. On Monday a wealthy eccentric insisted her dog was the reincarnation of her deceased husband and nothing Ann said could change her mind. On Wednesday, a man was adamant that he was Cleopatra in a past life and wanted Ann's confirmation so his therapist would finally believe him. Finally, today, to finish off the week, the selfie reading. What Ann needed now was a light meal and a cold glass of sauvignon blanc.

#

The four friends were seated at a table Michael had reserved for them at Scarpetta. He toasted with champagne, "To great friends." Their conversations flowed easily. Michael and Steve talked about their day at the convention. Allison and Meg chatted about the ambiance of the restaurant, life in their respective cities, how each couple had met, and their careers.

Meg asked Allison about her book, *Psychic Awareness*. "How on Earth did you decide on that topic?"

"Here's the short version of a very long story. I wanted to write about people who claimed to be psychic." Allison paused, "In the process of my research, I learned that there were more frauds, enthusiastic over-the-top nutcases, and well-meaning incompetents than those who possessed a highly developed sixth sense. The over-abundance of con artists and their schemes provided me with plenty of material for my book."

Michael jumped into the conversation. "Allison, why don't you tell Meg about your television show?"

"I'm sure she doesn't want to hear my life story the first time we meet," Allison chided.

"Please go on, Allison," Meg said. "I'd love to hear about your show."

"Actually, it was only a series of segments on the evening news." Allison explained how her research on psychics for her book caught the attention of a television executive. That led to Allison having her segments on the news where she exposed the charlatans and how they perpetrated their acts of deception. "The mail we received gave us great feedback. Most viewers appreciated the insights. However, the topic did attract some, let me be politically correct, mentally unstable persons."

Steve reached for Allison's hand, "And, my wife almost got killed in the process. She was stalked by a lunatic fan of the show. Turns out he was a serial killer."

"This is the most fascinating dinner conversation I've had in quite a while, if ever," Meg said.

"I guess I should have warned you," Michael laughed.

"Allison . . . you still with us?" Steve teased. "What's got your attention?"

"What?" Allison said staring off.

"Would you like to give the waiter your order?" Steve prompted-ed.

"Oh, I'm sorry." Allison gave her order then turned to Steve who was reading the menu and trying to decide between the ravioli and the gnocchi. "I think I know that woman." Allison motioned toward the entrance of the restaurant.

"Who?"

"The blonde woman in the gray dress. Right there."

The young waiter in the ill-fitted tuxedo jacket glanced toward the woman Allison had indicated.

"She's so familiar," Allison commented. "I think she's a sorority sister."

"Oh, that's Miss Paxton," the waiter added, "she's one of my regular customers. I'm so sorry. I couldn't help but overhear. I didn't mean to intrude in your conversation."

"That's okay," Allison said to the embarrassed waiter. Then questioned him, "Miss Paxton?"

"Yes, she's a really nice lady and lives in the building next door."

#

Ann waited at the maître d' station for Kurtz to escort her to her table. Soft Italian music played in the background while people chatted. A powerful pull diverted her attention to two couples engrossed in conversation near the windows. She gaped in disbelief. There sat Allison Rogers!

#

Allison saw the woman back away and lost sight of her in the group of people waiting to be seated. "She looks like . . . no, that's not who I thought it was."

Michael sensed there was more to Allison's observation than a sorority sister lookalike.

Steve appeared not to notice his wife's reaction and gave his order to the waiter. The guys continued to discuss the new light-weight weapons the Israelis demonstrated. Throughout the meal, the men talked about the new 'toys' like excited school boys. Over

122

dessert, Meg asked about the stalker who Steve had mentioned.

Allison seemed reluctant to tell the story but gave a quick over-view of the madman who became an obsessed fan when she was on television. He claimed they were both crusaders for the innocent and were kindred souls. "The difference was that I was exposing con artists and he was the man known as the Stone Killer."

Steve added, "The bottom line is that my wife is here today, and that psycho ended up a crispy critter in a public garage stairwell."

Meg gasped.

"On that note," Steve said, "Michael and I have an early break-fast meeting and a lecture on forensic techniques at the convention center tomorrow. This has been a fun evening, but all good things have to come to an end. How about we pick up where we left off, tomorrow."

CHAPTER TWENTY-EIGHT

The lobby in the building where the waiter said Ms. Paxton lived, was kinetic with a cacophony of sounds. High heels clicked on the marble floors, people engaged in phone conversations, a frazzled dog walker struggled to keep her charges from barking at everyone as she walked them through the busy space.

Allison stood at the front desk. She cleared her throat to get the attention of the concierge who appeared more focused on the commotion the three small dogs made than on Allison. "Excuse me," Allison raised her voice so the man would hear her. "Would you please call Ms. Paxton and let her know that Allison Rogers is here. She's expecting me."

"Certainly, Ma'am." He dialed and waited. "Good morning, Ms. Paxton. This is Hilmer at the front desk. Ms. Allison Rogers is here. She said you're expecting her. Shall I send her up?" His demeanor changed. "I understand. Yes, very well."

He hung up and turned to Allison. "I'm sorry, Ma'am. Um . . . Ms. Paxton is not at home and is out of town indefinitely. I'll be glad to leave her a note that you were here."

"No, thank you. That won't be necessary. She knows how to reach me."

\#

Michael hated the traffic congestion at the Philadelphia International Airport but he wouldn't allow Steve and Allison to take a cab from their hotel. The abrupt airport cops directing traffic must have trained with the Gestapo. Michael barely had time to say goodbye to his friends, get their luggage out and on to the curb before the Uniforms blew their whistles and threatened tickets if he didn't, "Move that car, NOW!"

"Bonjour, boss," Sylvie greeted Michael when he returned to the office.

"Sylvie, I picked up something for you on my way back from the airport." Michael placed the small waxed paper bag with a soft Philly pretzel inside, on her desk. "I thought you might enjoy one. Here's some mustard packets if you need them."

"Merci, boss!" *Ring, ring.* "S.H.I., Sylvie speaking. I'll check for you." Sylvie put the call on hold. "Before you walk away," she handed him several slips of pink paper with phone messages on them, "take these with you. As usual, they're all urgent." She winked.

At his desk, Michael sorted the messages and prepared to return the priority calls when his phone vibrated. It was an (813) area code but he didn't recognize the number. "Michael Vega."

"Hi. It's Allison," she spoke above a whisper.

"Is everything okay?"

"Yes. We're still in the airport. I can't talk long. Steve thinks I'm in the ladies' room."

"Did you leave something in the car?"

"No. I need to ask you for a favor. But, before I tell you what it is," Allison sounded stressed, "I need to know that for the time being, this conversation stays between the two of us."

"Okay . . . what do you need?" Michael wasn't fazed when he heard Allison's confession about the woman she saw in the restaurant. Allison suspected she was the mastermind who was behind the Stone Killer murders in Florida. The gruesome homicides occurred while Michael was on the Tampa police force, although he wasn't involved in the case. The killer was responsible for murders across the state of Florida. The common thread in all the cases was that each victim had escaped justice through the legal system. One case Michael recalled was that of a pedophile the killer hog-tied, dragged through the swamp, and staked face down on the bank of an alligator infested lake. There was little evidence left behind.

Newspaper clippings of the murders were found tacked to the wall of the killer's bedroom, the word 'Karma' written across each article, and forensic evidence that connected him to several events were found in the garage.

Allison filled Michael in on her suspicions about the woman at the restaurant last night. "Michael, there's no doubt in my mind she was Anne Preston, the psychic I met in Florida. I believed she was the puppet master who directed the Stone killer. By the time I had collected evidence to connect her with the killer and convinced the police, she had disappeared. Her car was found submerged in Tampa Bay. Her purse, with a sizeable amount of cash inside, her identification, and luggage were in the car. Her body was never recovered. From what Steve told me, there was no further credit card or bank activity and nothing on her social security number. I always felt it was a staged accident. Since the police had who they believed was the Stone Killer, they didn't pursue Anne Preston's possible connection." Allison had to end the call when she heard their flight announcement.

There was little information to go on, but Michael would do a rudimentary background check on Ann Paxton, the woman Allison saw at the Philadelphia restaurant and suspected was Anne Preston who vanished in Florida. He was uncomfortable that Allison wanted to keep this a secret from her husband but understood she didn't want to upset him unnecessarily. Her indirect involvement in the Stone Killer case nearly cost his wife, her life. If Ann Paxton was, who Allison suspected, it could reopen the case.

The background check on Ann Paxton revealed no arrest history, nor any military record. She left Ohio after high school. Her Ohio Driver's License expired in the 1980's. No other license was issued under her name until she moved to Pennsylvania less than two years ago. No employment records except the business license that was obtained around the same time for an office on Walnut Street where she does consultations. She has a residence at Rittenhouse Square.

No marriage record was found.

It was a possibility that she had been out of the country during the unaccounted- for gap in time. Michael hated to do it, but since he didn't have access to her passport status, he called the former businessman he did a job for in Orlando, the newly elected congressman friend of Connor's. The Pennington photos that Michael obtained while he was on the job in Orlando had saved him a shitload of money in his divorce settlement. He was more than happy to provide the passport information Michael requested.

What Michael found proved nothing, but, unless Ann Paxton was abducted by aliens and spent most of her life on a flying saucer with a robot named Klaatu, there's a big piece of the puzzle that's missing.

#

"Hi Allison. Got a minute?"

"Sure Michael. I'm just leaving the gym."

"I did that check on your friend, Ann Paxton."

"Believe me, Michael, she's no friend."

Michael filled Allison in on all the details he had gleaned from his research.

"Either way, Allison, she's clean . . . maybe a little too clean. It's too soon to jump to any conclusions but I'll say this, I'm a bit baffled."

CHAPTER TWENTY-NINE

A distraught Jane was on the phone with Ann and recounted the story of Zack Davis whose brutally beaten body had been found stuffed in a cardboard box filled with trash. Jane told Ann that she suspected he was the same sickly child she spoke with in the park recently and now she was overwhelmed with guilt that she hadn't reported the bruises she saw on him, to the police.

Jane said that two days before the child was reported missing Zack's father married his fiancé, Gloria. His father was eager to submit to a polygraph and passed but Gloria refused to take one.

Unbeknown to Jane, Ann had followed the story and was aware that Child Protective Services had been called to the home several times but reports of neglect or abuse were never filed and Zack and his older sister remained in the home. This particular story had riled Ann's sense of injustice. She had planned to do her own research on the murder of this boy. Jane told Ann she felt compelled to attend the public service and asked Ann to attend the memorial with her for moral support. Ann could be there for her sister and also have the opportunity to psychically read the family of the child.

#

Jane and Ann stood outside of the stone archway entrance to Fairmount Park. Strangers undeterred by the blustery cold day gathered at the makeshift memorial where Zack's body was found. An elderly man handed out white balloons to the influx of people who approached. Zack's father stood in front of the group in obvious emotional distress. Gloria, the father's new wife, attempted to comfort him while the girl who stood between them, clung to her father with a look of terror on her face.

Some mourners, moved by emotion, wept while Zack's father spoke about his son. Jane brushed away a tear from her cheek. Two undercover police officers mingled with the people and scrutinized the activity. To Ann, they stood out like sore thumbs, but no one else seemed to pay attention to them. The crowd fell silent as a petite, dark-skinned woman bundled against the cold began to sing <u>Amazing Grace</u> in a powerful voice, much larger than her tiny stature would suggest. The Channel 7 cameraman panned the crowd. Ann stepped closer to Jane and used her scarf to shield her face from being televised but didn't take her eyes off Gloria.

Ann was able to confirm what she had already suspected. The father's grief was genuine and laced with guilt, but Gloria's act of innocence couldn't fool Ann. She knew what Gloria had done to Zack. Ann also knew how this would end for Gloria.

#

It was a slow weekend at the office and Michael's first couple of days off in a while. Stretched out on the couch while the Penn State football game was on tv, he drifted off to sleep. The room was dark when Michael woke except for the light from the tv. He was astounded that he slept through the end of the football game and that the late news had started.

He sat up and stopped in the middle of a loud yawn when he heard the anchor woman say, "The word 'Karma' prominently displayed at the scene has police speculating that this could be the work of a vigilante." We'll be back with the details after this break."

Karma? Michael sat back down and waited.

The reporter led with the story. "The body of Gloria Hancock Davis, a person of interest in the murder of her eight-year-old stepson Zack Davis, was discovered today by a homeless man who found a purse that contained her identification, next to a large cardboard box at a construction site in the vicinity of where Zack Davis' body was discovered. The man then discovered her body wrapped in a blanket inside the box. The police spokesman said the preliminary cause of death appears to be blunt force trauma. The word 'Karma' was written on the outside of the box in what appeared to be blood."

Michael recalled his conversation with Allison and her suspicions about Ann Paxton, the connection between the word 'karma' and the Stone Killer in Florida. He figured it might be a good idea to have Sylvie set up an appointment for him to have a consultation with Ann Paxton, but before that happened, he wanted to take a more in depth look at her life including her missing background.

As he initially informed Allison, Ann Paxton had a clean record. But, he thought, what were the chances of two so-called psychics having the same initials, the same first name, the same body stature, the same age, and Allison said she received a crystal paperweight she believed was from Ann Preston. The package was postmarked from Philadelphia and dated around the same time Ann Paxton shows up in town. And now, the word 'karma' at a murder scene.

The threads of coincidence had begun to weave an odd fabric of suspicion.

Michael looked at the clock. It was late. "What the hell." He dialed the number.

"H-e-l-l-o?" a groggy voice answered.

"George, I know it's late–,"

"Aw, man. This better be good. I was in the middle of such an awesome dream. I was just about to—,"

"Hold on, George. I need a favor, bro. I want you to work a job up here for me. It might take a couple of weeks, if you can take off that long?"

"Sure. When do you need me?"

"ASAP. I'm doing this off the books for a friend."

"You got it. I'll book my flight for Friday. We're supposed to have Tio Armando's birthday dinner at Mom's tomorrow. You know how she'd react if I didn't show up."

CHAPTER THIRTY

At the airport curbside loading zone, Michael hugged his brother and tossed his luggage on the backseat. "It's good to see you George."

A rotund airport cop waived his arms and shouted at them to keep moving. Michael waited in the loading zone while a group of Asian pedestrians wheeled their suitcases in front of his car. The cop shouted at them to 'use the marked walkway and to move it along.' From the expression on their faces, Michael doubted they gave a crap about what he said.

Michael navigated his way through the airport traffic and headed toward South Philadelphia. "We'll go to the office but first I'm taking you to a Philly landmark for the best cheese steak you're ever going to eat. I hope you're hungry."

"I don't know. I'm pretty full from that bag of peanuts they gave me on the flight."

They devoured their cheesesteaks and caught up on family news, Michael's girlfriend, Meg, George's chaotic love life, and the recent hiring of the new coach for the Tampa Bay Buccaneers.

On their way to the office, Michael gave George an overview of the case that involved Ann Paxton /Anne Preston and his client's suspicion that they are the same person. "To be honest, it's an old friend's wife who insists that this woman was involved in the Stone Killer murders in Florida."

"I remember that case!" George said. "The papers said the killer was the judge, jury, and executioner. I just thought he was another screwed-up psychopath. I mean . . . who feeds a living person to alligators or makes a human torch out of some drunk?" George paused. "Christ, he cut off a woman's head and threw it into Tampa Bay! Man, that's sick shit."

"Damn, Bro, I'm impressed." Michael was shocked that his brother knew so much about the murders.

"Don't be. I'm not one of those nutty serial killer groupies, Michael. That asshole screwed up a hot and heavy romance I had. It was the best time of my life. That girl had the greatest tits I ever saw."

"So, what happened to *this* love of your life?" Michael chided.

"She freaked out and moved to North Dakota to be with her family when the lawyer she worked for was murdered by the sicko. She was afraid she'd be next. So much for true love."

Michael drove past the vacant spot designated for Connor Johns and parked next to it. Inside the building, George stopped in front of the antique bell in the lobby.

"George, it doesn't look like it, but over a hundred years ago this used to be a firehouse. Connor was a history buff and insisted on keeping this bell."

"I don't remember a lot about him, Michael, just that Mom would chase him and Dad outside so Connor could smoke his cigar." George put his hand on his brother's back. "You knew him a lot better than I did. I know you took his death pretty hard."

"Yeah, I did. But I swear sometimes he hangs around here. Every once in a while, I get a good whiff of his cigar."

Like a proud big brother, Michael gave George a tour of the building and introduced him to his staff. They spent the rest of the afternoon in Michael's office and discussed the case George would be working.

"So, let me get this right. You want me to spy on a psychic that your client says is a psych-O." George shook his head and smirked. "Cool."

"Don't get carried away, George. You'll be more of a sleuth, than a spy."

There was a tap at the door. "Excuse me, boss. I thought you and your brother might like some refreshments." Sylvie left the tray that included beverages, condiments, and snacks on the desk and turned to leave.

"Sylvie, you're a mind reader or you heard my stomach grumble." George called after her as he reached for a sandwich, "You're the best."

"Merci," she said before she closed the door.

Michael handed George a napkin and then an enlarged driver's license photograph of the subject. "This is the only picture we can find of Ann Paxton, but it's recent. A buddy of Connor's on the force here in Philly faxed it to me. I told him I was working a cold case–a possible homicide. He's old school and knew I wouldn't drop Connor's name if it wasn't important."

George studied the photograph as Michael slid a sheet of paper in front of his brother. "And this is what I found on Paxton after she left high school until she appeared years later in Philadelphia." Michael laughed at the puzzlement on his brother's face. "What, you don't like a challenge?" The paper was blank.

It was late when they finished laying out the plan to track Ann Paxton. Everyone in the office had gone home for the day. There was an eerie quiet in the building.

They prepared to leave when the lights flickered off and on. Off and on.

The expression on George's face spoke volumes.

"It's an old building," Michael said. Just then, Connor's derringer cigarette lighter that Michael kept on his desk, fell to the floor.

Now George looked spooked.

"I probably bumped the desk with my briefcase," Michael placated. He locked the door behind them and laughed at George who hurried through the lobby. A few steps toward the door, Michael caught the sudden strong aroma of cigar smoke.

CHAPTER THIRTY-ONE

Bundled in cold weather gear which he had to borrow from his brother, George left Michael's office. It had been quite some time since he visited a northern state in the winter and his old Pea Coat and gloves weren't enough to fend off the elements. He braced himself against the blast of bitter cold air and got into one of the company cars which was kept behind the building and out of eyeshot from passersby. While George waited for the car to warm, he reviewed his notes on the strategy that he and Michael had laid out to observe Ann Paxton.

George's attention was focused on inputting Ann's address into his GPS when he was startled by a *tap tap* on the window. Sylvie held out a thermos. George rolled down the window just as a frigid gust of wind hit him in the face. *Shit, it's freezin'!*

"Sylvie, what are you doing here this early in the morning?"

"I thought you might like some hot cocoa." Sylvie handed him the silver thermos and darted for the office.

"I love you, Sylvie!" George yelled.

Parked in a discreet location, George had a direct line of sight to the exit of the garage under Ann Paxton's building. It was a good assumption that she wouldn't walk anywhere on a day like this.

#

The morning weather report warned of an approaching nor'easter expected to hit the tomorrow. It was forecasted to last a couple of days. Although Ann appreciated the peaceful quiet that

135

accompanied the fresh snowfall, she would miss the revenue from her clients who had already begun to reschedule their appointments in anticipation of the bad weather.

She stood at the window and sipped from her cup of herbal tea while she looked at the overcast sky, barren Sycamore trees, and the few people on the square who were bundled to stave off the chill . . . for her, the starkness of the scene gave her a sense of tranquility; a rare experience. She enjoyed her solitude. As far back as Ann could remember she didn't have the need nor the desire to cultivate personal relationships. She never thought of herself as a pessimist, rather a realist. Her atypical perception of people allowed her to see them as they actually were; narcissistic, phony, and cruel. Those who were not were the exception, like her sister Jane.

This year was the first time since they were children that the sisters would spend the holidays together. Ann planned to drive to the King of Prussia Mall to buy something special for Jane and for an obligatory gift for Gary. The more time Ann had spent in his presence, the more she'd come to dislike him, but it was important that Jane didn't suspect Ann's disdain toward Gary.

She dressed and headed to her car in the underground garage. On winter days like today, she appreciated how fast the seat warmers worked. A few minutes later, she was on the road. Ann turned on the radio. Christmas music played. God how she hated carols. She turned off the radio. Silence was preferable.

#

George picked up his digital recorder and spoke into it. "9:47 am. Subject left garage of her residence driving a dark blue Lexus. We are entering the Schuylkill Expressway, heading west." He returned the recorder to the center console.

#

Traffic was heavier than Ann anticipated. She assumed more shoppers were out today stocking up on supplies before the storm. Ann slowed the car to take the exit for a secondary road which led to the mall. As she rounded the exit, she caught a glimpse of an expansive Colonial-style house set back from the road. The driveway was lined with skeletal trees which Ann imagined in full green regalia during the summer. *Tara!* In an instant Ann was taken back to her youth—to the times she would read to Jane until she'd fall asleep.

"Moron!" Her car was forced off the road by a driver who was texting. She blasted the horn and steered back onto the road.

#

In order to maintain his cover, George slowed his vehicle until the Lexus was back on to the road. He drove by her car and then another before moving into the right lane. He slowed his speed which forced the line of traffic behind him to pass. The subject was again ahead of him.

#

Her agitation subsided when she saw the turnoff to the mall. Ann glanced into her right-side mirror then clicked on her turn signal.

A chill washed over her despite the heat in the car. She sensed something amiss and looked around, not sure who or what she expected to see. She saw nothing suspicious and shook off the feeling, attributing it to the jerkoff who almost smashed into her a few minutes ago.

Ann found an open spot to park near an entrance to the mall. At least when she was done shopping, she wouldn't have to trek far in the cold with an armful of packages.

The over-abundant display of artificial Christmas trees that lined the center court of the mall seemed obscenely commercial. Each was decorated in a motif more elaborate than the next. The signs indicated they were to be sold to benefit The Children's Charity. She would be amazed if any of the money they collected would be used for the children.

#

George jogged past rows of cars and headed toward the mall entrance. He paused in between the double glass doors, unwrapped the plaid scarf from around his neck, removed his gloves, gray cap, and Pea Coat, all the while he kept the subject in sight.

#

Aware she was being watched, Ann looked around and caught a young man sizing her up. Their eyes met.

"Miss, you look like someone who would appreciate the beauty of these masterpieces. You're obviously a woman of good taste." His salacious greeting matched his flamboyant outfit, made complete with a hot pink scarf. "Would you care to purchase a tree . . . it's for The Children's Charity?" asked the twenty-something salesman.

"No, thank you," Ann replied, "but they are pretty."

"A donation would be pretty, too. I'm sure if you peek in that fabulous designer bag of yours you'll find a little extra cash."

He had no reaction to Ann's look of contempt. She turned to leave and heard him say to the older well-dressed couple she passed as she walked away, "You look like someone who would appreciate the beauty of these masterpieces. You're obviously . . ."

Soon after Ann left Neiman Marcus with perfume and a burgundy silk sweater for Jane, a Lee Child book for Gary, and the perfect Italian leather boots for herself, she bought hot Chai tea at a kiosk and sat on a nearby bench to take a break.

#

Not far from the subject, George stopped at a Christmas apparel booth where he kept her in view. He browsed through the merchandise then purchased a red knit cap emblazoned with a Santa on the front. He tugged the hat down over his ears.

#

Ann finished her beverage, gathered her packages, and walked in the direction of the exit near the decorated trees. A child squealed with glee, "Mommy, Mommy, this is the one! Take my picture. Take my picture, please!" Ann turned to see a little girl posed in front of a tree trimmed with silver and gold ornaments, and peacock feathers. The coat the child wore was too small and had seen better days. But, her eyes were bright and she giggled with delight at the beauty of the tree. Her mother, dressed only in a faded sweater and jeans, hurried to take a few pictures then snapped her phone shut.

"Lady, do you want to buy this tree," the snooty young salesman asked, "or just take pictures of it?" He looked down his nose and glared at the woman and her child.

"I'm sorry," the mother lowered her eyes. "We didn't touch anything."

The little girl blurted, "This is the one I'm going to show my friends at school. I'm going to pretend it's mine. We can't have one 'cause we live in a—"

"Come on Becky, we're late." The mother's face flushed as she took her daughter's hand and hurried to the exit.

Ann situated her packages at her feet, rummaged through her purse, opened her wallet and removed five, one-hundred-dollar bills. She transferred the contents of a small bag to another, folded the money and placed it inside the small gift bag then stuffed tissue paper on top. She gathered her parcels and walked over to the obnoxious man who was in the midst of his spiel to yet another potential donor. She stopped to face him and interrupted his rehearsed presentation.

"You are a sad excuse for a human being. How dare you try to raise money for a charity when you have no concept of what that word means. The way you embarrassed that woman and her little girl—your mother must be so-o-o proud of you."

The salesman stood red-faced, the customer scurried away into the mass of shoppers.

Ann kept the woman and child in sight as they left the mall. Snow had begun and covered cars and the asphalt. Regardless of the forecasted storm tomorrow, Mother Nature seemed to have her own schedule. Ann walked past her car and through the maze of vehicles to the far edge of the lot when she caught up to them. The child had already climbed into the car which was filled with boxes and clothes. It was obvious that the car was their home.

Ann approached the woman. "Excuse me?"

The mother spun around. "We didn't do anything wrong," a touch of fear in her voice.

"Of course, you didn't." Ann handed the gift bag to the mother. "Merry Christmas."

#

George had put in a long and boring day of surveillance and recorded copious notes. When he checked in with Michael who told him to call it a day, George didn't hesitate to return to the office.

Michael asked, "Anything of interest happen?"

"Pretty routine. But I'll tell ya, you've got some shitty drivers around here. Some dick almost ran her off the road. I thought my assignment was going to end early." George deposited the digital recorder on the desk. "I'll give her credit, she kept control of her car."

Michael put the recorder in a desk drawer. "Sylvie will transcribe this in the morning." Michael handed him another recorder and said, "You can use this one tomorrow."

As if on cue, Sylvie entered, smiled at Michael and placed a tray of sandwiches on his desk. "I'll bet neither of you have eaten all day.

Now, don't let me find this food still here in the morning. Good-night, boss."

George whispered, "How does she always know what we need?"

"I'm still trying to figure that one out myself. Even Connor wondered if she was clairvoyant. Personally, I don't care if she is or if she has the office bugged. It works."

#

With arms full of packages, Ann stepped off the elevator and fumbled for her keys. That's when she heard the familiar *click* of Mrs. Bolinski's lock and the door open.

"Oh, hello, Ms. Paxton. I see you've been shopping and at Neiman Marcus no less. How nice. Did they have any good sales? They must have. I see you have plenty of bags. You must have bought out half the store. I love Neiman's, but my husband hates to shop with me." The closer Ann got to her own front door, the louder Mrs. Bolinski's voice rose. "Maybe the next time you go, I can go with you and . . ."

"Nice talking to you, Mrs. Bolinski. Have a good evening," Ann waved and stepped inside her condo. She leaned against the closed door. "Doesn't that woman ever take a breath?"

CHAPTER THIRTY-TWO

Michael made it a practice to show up early to work which allowed him time without the distractions of the usual office chaos, to catch up on paperwork. The building was cold and eerily quiet. An aroma of cigar smoke wafted around him and he imagined Connor seated at his desk smoking his cohiba.

Slow to start the review of invoices, the part of his job that he disliked, he couldn't procrastinate any longer and got to work. Deep in thought, Michael was startled when the office door opened.

"Bonjour, boss." Sylvie handed Michael a stack of files.

"Bonjour, Sylvie. Como ça va?"

"Ça va bien! Very nice, boss. I'm doing very well, thank you for asking."

Michael shrugged. "I'm learning, Sylvie."

Sylvie chuckled as she left the room.

The accounting completed, Michael turned his attention to the folder on top of the pile. It was marked, "Paxton, Ann." Two weeks of shadowing revealed Ann Paxton's routine was unremarkable compared to the information Allison had given him regarding Anne Preston/Serial Killer in Florida. He shook his head. He knew George stuck with procedure protocol. It would be unlike him to miss anything. George would have picked up anything suspicious. There was nothing that tied Ann Paxton of Philadelphia to the Anne Preston in Florida, other than their physical descriptions and careers. Yet, his instinct told him there was something more. But what?

Disappointed as Allison might be, Michael couldn't fabricate facts. He made the call to her.

Allison answered on the second ring. "Good morning, Michael. I was just about to call you!"

"Guess I beat you to it." Michael took a deep breath. "I have the Paxton report in front of me. I'm sorry to say it doesn't confirm your suspicions. We had eyes on her for weeks. I agree with you that her background check was questionable, but there's nothing more in this report that would lead anyone to believe she's anything but an average citizen."

"You've got to be kidding, Michael. I'm positive that—"

"I have the report in my hand as we speak, Allison . . . she goes to work and back home; she goes shopping and back home, she goes out to eat, alone, and goes back home, alone."

"That can't be all, Michael."

"Nevertheless, there was no unusual behavior, nothing inappropriate at all."

Allison's silence was deafening.

Michael spoke first. "I know this isn't the result you expected, Allison, and I get no pleasure in conveying it to you. Trust me on this. I assure you this won't be the last time I check on her."

"I appreciate that, Michael. I know you put a lot of time into this."

Michael heard the frustration in her voice. "Allison, if I find the slightest indication of criminal activity, you'll be the second call I make."

It wasn't the first time Michael had to say to someone, 'the bad news is, I didn't find anything,' and 'the good news is, I didn't find anything.' Yet, he had a nagging suspicion that the topic of Ann Paxton would return before long.

#

Michael left the jewelry store with a small black velvet box in hand and a smile on his face. He headed home to pick up George for their dinner with Meg tonight before they took George to the airport.

Michael stopped the car curbside at his apartment, blew the horn, and smirked as George struggled with his roller bag and a humungous potted poinsettia as he made his way to the car.

He stifled a laugh as George fumbled with the oversized plant and tried to set it on the floor of the backseat.

"What?" George asked. "It's for Meg."

"Merry Christmas," Meg exclaimed, when she opened the door and welcomed Michael and George into her home. She beamed when she saw her gift from George.

The inside of Meg's apartment looked like a Norman Rockwell painting. There were stockings hung on the mantle. One was included for George. The Christmas tree was decorated with old fashioned ornaments, lights, and tinsel. The dining room table was set for a holiday feast.

George took in a deep breath, and said, "No way! Is that turkey I smell?"

"Guys, I know it's a few days early, but I made a Christmas dinner for you." Meg handed them glasses of eggnog. "I wanted to make sure you two could celebrate the holiday together since George is headed back to Florida tonight."

Sated with turkey, stuffing, and all the trimmings, Michael sat back and listened to George entertain Meg with his animated and somewhat embellished stories of their childhood. He talked about the time their family took a camping trip deep in the mountains of Georgia.

"Early in the morning, Michael left the tent and walked into the woods but neglected to take toilet paper with him. The smooth, shiny leaves he used instead, turned out to be poison ivy. For two weeks, he walked like a bowlegged cowboy."

Meg laughed until she couldn't catch her breath.

Michael pretended to be incensed but he too broke out in side-splitting laughter. "Just remember, George, paybacks are hell!"

George raised his hands in surrender.

"Michael, you never told me how funny your brother is." Meg

wiped tears of laughter from her face. "You two behave while I'm gone. I hope you like Tres Leches cake."

"Are you kidding me? It's my favorite!" George said. When Meg left the room, "You know Michael, she's a keeper."

"I'm glad you think so, too. I don't know how I got so lucky." Michael pushed his chair back from the table. "After that fiasco with Teresa . . . well, I thought I was done with marriage."

"Bro, are you saying what I think you're saying?"

"Yeah, I guess I am. I wanted you to be the first to know, and if she says yes, I'd like you to be my best man. I'm going to ask her tonight after we drop you at the airport."

CHAPTER THIRTY-THREE

"CODE BLUE, ER. CODE BLUE, ER," blared over the intercom.

A distraught elderly woman who clutched her husband's bloody coat tight to her chest, was hurried out of his emergency room cubicle as a stream of medical personnel rushed in, with Dr. Gary Mara and his nurse, Karen Chapman on his heels. Each performed their duty with care, but due to the patient's extensive head injuries and failed heart, time of death was called.

The police officer who came from the scene of the accident, waited in the hall. Dr. Mara told the officer that the patient had expired.

The cop shook his head. "So many people affected by two reckless delinquents who thought it'd be fun to steal a car and speed through a neighborhood. Instead of a prank, these two brothers are facing a murder charge."

"If you'll excuse me," Dr. Mara said, "I have to go talk to the family."

It had been a difficult shift in the emergency room, in addition to the customary broken bones, stitches, bumps and bruises, there were too many senseless incidents; a toddler left inside a car died of hypothermia; an unlicensed drunk driver hit a family of five, head-on; and, three fentanyl overdoses.

Dr. Mara sat in the alcove designated for doctors to record patient reports when nurse Chapman walked up behind him, leaned close and whispered something in his ear, rubbed her breasts against his back, and walked away.

He grinned, finished his final report, and left for the day.

CHAPTER THIRTY-FOUR

"Thanks for coming in on your day off," the head nurse said to Karen Chapman. "You know how hectic it gets in here around the holidays. It's been crazy all day and with the flu going around, we're short-handed."

Karen sat through report and requested to be assigned to Mrs. Spaulding, the patient who's twenty-four-weeks pregnant in room twelve who slipped off a step-stool while decorating her Christmas tree. "I'm familiar with Mrs. Spaulding," Karen mentioned to the charge nurse. "She was my patient last month when she came in with the complaint of severe nausea."

"That's a good idea, Karen." The charge nurse made a notation on her iPad. "Mrs. Spaulding is an apprehensive patient and a familiar nurse would be comforting to her."

Room twelve was on the opposite side of the ER. Karen nodded to the ward clerk, took the mobile computer that sat outside the patient's room, and opened the curtain. "Mrs. Spaulding, I'm Karen Chapman. I'm going to be your nurse this afternoon." She glanced at the notes and the doctor's orders that were entered into the system.

Mrs. Spaulding said, "I remember you from when I was here before. You were so kind to me." The young patient started to cry. "Is my baby going to be okay? My husband told me to wait until he got home to trim the tree, but I wanted to surprise him." She nervously bit her lip. "He's going to be so mad at me."

"Mrs. Spaulding, I'm reading the doctor's notes. It looks like you've sprained your wrist but everything else appears normal, however, the doctor ordered lab work just to be on the safe side. The phlebotomist should be up shortly to take your blood, meantime," Karen handed her a small plastic jar, "can you give me a urine sample now? You can leave the jar in the bathroom when you're finished."

Mrs. Spaulding returned to her bed and Karen charted her vital signs. The lab tech came in to perform the blood draw. Karen went into the patient's bathroom, removed another specimen jar from her pocket, poured half of Mrs. Spaulding's urine into that jar, tightened the lid, wrote on the label, and slipped that container back into her pocket. She stepped out of the bathroom and said to the technician, "Patty, here's Mrs. Spaulding's urine sample." She put a scantily filled specimen jar on the lab tech's cart and left the room.

With her hand pressed to her pocket, Karen took the stairs to the second floor and walked hurriedly through the hallways and into the lab. "David, I'm so happy it's you on duty today," she said to the obese man. "I have a big favor to ask," she said, a little out of breath.

"Well, hello to you too!" he said, playful annoyance evident in his greeting.

"I'm sorry, David. I only have a minute." She handed him the specimen jar that contained the portion of Mrs. Spaulding's urine sample.

The technician read Karen's name on the label. "This is yours?"

Karen nodded and smiled coyly. "I know it's not normal procedure, but I need you to run a pregnancy test."

"Well, I don't know." He sighed, pushed his glasses up onto his bald head and hesitated. "This is highly irregular. You know we both could get into trouble." He rubbed his temple. "Why don't you just pee on a stick?"

"I did several times, and it was positive. But you know those EPT's aren't always accurate." She pleaded, "Please, David, I'm so excited I just can't wait to find out for sure."

He lowered his glasses to his nose and said, "Consider this my Christmas present to you . . . but don't ask me for any more favors." He winked at her.

"You're angel, David! Call me when you have the results."

\#

Karen paced between the living room and dining room, her phone at her ear and a glass of vodka in her hand.

". . . Yes, I understand, but you said you were going to tell her you were on-call so we could have a couple of hours together tonight.

". . . But I have a special Christmas present for you.

". . . Not that, silly. Something else. Something you won't get from her.

". . . Gary, do you realize that we don't even have our Thursday dinners together anymore?

". . . Of course, I'm disappointed. It's Christmas Eve and I'm alone, again.

". . . I know you're sorry, but that doesn't change anything.

". . . Yes, I forgive you. But promise you'll make time for me tomorrow. Even if it's only an hour.

". . . Goodnight. I love you too. I'll see you tomorrow."

She reached into the freezer, grabbed the bottle of vodka, and carried it into the living room. Karen plopped on to the sofa and refilled her glass. Her Persian cat jumped on her lap and began to purr. "Aw Coco, at least you're here with me." She stroked the cat's thick fur then took a swallow of the clear, cold liquid.

Karen's eyes filled with tears as she admired the artificial tree. "It is perfect but it's fake, just like everything in my life." She took another sip of her drink. Tears spilled down her face. "It's just you and me again, Coco." She finished the drink and refilled her glass. Karen reached for the remote control and switched on the television. Jimmy Stewart stood at the side of a bridge while he contemplated his life and 'ending it all.'

"Oh, my sweet Coco, I know y-o-o-u would miss me if I was gone, but would Gary? No-o-o, he has a wifey, but not for l-o-o-ng," her guttural laugh sounded like a wounded animal, "not after my surrr-prrrise tomorrow!"

Karen raised her glass in the air, "Here's to y-o-o-o-u, Mrs. Spaulding."

CHAPTER THIRTY-FIVE

It was a clear, crisp morning which filled Jane with the promise of a perfect holiday. The morning sun reflected off the blanket of snow that had fallen overnight. It was unusual for Gary to sleep late but today was one of his rare days off and not on-call. Jane woke early to prepare a Christmas breakfast for him. The final touch to her presentation was to put a single rose in a budvase and place it on the wicker tray.

Dishes on the tray rattled as Jane made her way up the staircase to their bedroom and heard Gary awake and talking to someone in a guarded, subdued tone. She opened the double-doors to their room and found him sitting on the edge of the bed with his phone to his ear.

Gary ended the call in an impersonal, almost abrupt manner. "Okay, you have a Merry Christmas too." Gary started to explain that the call was from a nurse and that he told her in no uncertain terms that he left instructions that he wasn't to be disturbed, that Dr. Goldberg was on call.

Jane overlooked the defensiveness she detected in his voice and chose not to comment on the call. She wouldn't allow anything to dampen her spirits, not today. She put the breakfast tray next to him on the bed. "Merry Christmas, sweetheart. I made the banana waffles you love."

"I don't feel like having waffles today, Jane," Gary sighed in exasperation. "I know you went to a lot of trouble, but you should have asked me first." He reached for the Santa mug. "I will take the coffee though."

The hurt she felt was palpable but Jane knew in her heart that he didn't do it on purpose. She understood that his need to control was part and parcel of being a doctor who had to make life and death decisions on a daily basis. No matter, she wasn't going to let his morning crankiness spoil her mood. "Come on Gary be happy, it's Christmas."

"I would've been happy if you'd brought me bacon and eggs. That's what I would have liked for breakfast. Oh yeah, but you won't cook bacon for me, will you?"

If you only knew why. . .

By mid-afternoon, more snow had begun to fall. In the kitchen, Jane busied herself preparing a pineapple glaze for the ham. Gary walked in. "Jane, can we start the day over?" He took her by the hand and led her into the living room where Jane had plugged in the Christmas lights and lit the logs in the fireplace. The sap in the wood crackled and the fragrance of the pine filled the room.

Gary remarked that that smell reminded him of the time he and his father trudged through the snow and into the woods to find and cut down their own tree for Christmas. On the way home, they stopped at a diner and had hot chocolate with marshmallows. As simple as that was, it was a freeze-frame memory that he would never forget. It was also the Christmas that his parents gave him his first microscope. That gift changed the rest of his life. He was eleven years old and knew he wanted to become a doctor.

It warmed Jane's heart to hear Gary speak with such sentiment. It was a rare occasion when he talked about his family or his past, for that matter.

The timer buzzed and spoiled the mood. Jane went to the kitchen and removed a casserole from the oven. When she returned, she found Gary sending a text. Without comment, he tucked his phone into his pant pocket.

Jane pretended not to notice and gave Gary his gift. He opened the box and exclaim, "Jane, it's the cashmere bathrobe I wanted. Thank you!"

He patted the sofa cushion and asked Jane to sit closer to him, placed a small square box decorated with a silver bow in her hand and said, "I hope you like this Jane. I designed it for you."

She opened the box. "Oh my gosh!" She held the crescent-shaped moon covered in pavé diamonds. A star ruby was set in the curve of the crescent. "It's beautiful, Gary." Jane jumped up, threw her arms around his neck, and kissed him.

Gary ignored the ping on his phone that signaled an incoming message.

#

On her way to Gary and Jane's for Christmas dinner, Ann drove behind a minivan for several blocks. It sported a large Christmas wreath attached to the back window. The vehicle turned into the driveway across the street from Jane's house. Ann drove into Jane's driveway, got out of the car, and caught sight of several children as they rushed out of the van, gifts in hand, to greet a white-haired woman who waited for them at the garland-draped front door. The children squealed with excitement, "Merry Christmas, Oma. We have presents for you!" It was a poignant scene, one Ann never experienced as a child. Until now, Ann had no use for Christmas. This year was different. Now she had a real family. She had Jane.

Ann contemplated, was it too late for her to move beyond her godforsaken past and live a normal life? Would someone one day relieve her of her duty to balance the scales of justice . . . was it even a possibility?

The excitement across the street quieted when the door to the neighbor's house closed. Ann grimaced. *Live a NORMAL life? Who am I kidding?* She walked to the back of the car and opened the lid revealing a shopping bag filled with several brightly wrapped packages.

Jane beamed with delight when she opened the door. "Ann, you're here!" She hugged her sister and kissed her cheek. "Let me help you with that," she reached for the bag. "Gary made his special hot spiced cider for us."

The bright and festive decorations were tastefully displayed. Jane's genuine welcome added to the coziness that pervaded the interior of the house. Tonight, Ann felt a true connection to family. But, with this newfound contentment came a shadow of trepidation deep from within. The cause . . . it was unclear.

"Here you go ladies, my world-famous Christmas drink." Gary handed the women cups of hot cider. The three of them opened their gifts to exclamations of 'It's just what I wanted,' 'I love it,' 'This is perfect.'

"Gary, Jane told me you designed that beautiful pendant. It's so unusual."

"Thank you," Gary said. "It's a unique gift for a unique wife. The Star Ruby matches the stars in her eyes."

"You're quite the romantic, Gary." Ann raised her glass and looked straight at him. "Here's to a devoted husband who appreciates his wife. Jane's a lucky girl." Ann knew the flush to Gary's face was not embarrassment at a compliment, but anger at her double-entendre.

Jane said, "I hope you're both hungry because dinner is ready."

It was a perfect evening of pleasant conversation and a delicious meal. Jane was ready to serve plum pudding when Gary's cell pinged. He excused himself and returned minutes later wearing his coat. "That was a text from Dr. Goldberg. I'm needed at the hospital. I shouldn't be long but don't wait up." Gary said goodnight and headed for the garage.

"Ann, I'm so sorry Gary had to leave. It was supposed to be his day off." Jane cut into the pudding and placed a dish in front of Ann. "But this is a doctor's life. Gary is such a dedicated physician. I don't know what the hospital would do without him."

While she listened to Jane's excuses for Gary's behavior, Ann nibbled at the plum pudding. She was aggravated and knew he wasn't going to work. Ann saw him for the bastard he was, but it was obvious that Jane loved him.

It was past midnight when Ann left their house and Gary had not yet returned. On her drive home, Ann's mood was as gray as the pewter sky. How could her sister not see through him? If she told Jane about the other woman would Jane blame her for destroying her 'perfect life?' Would Jane choose Gary over her? She wouldn't take that chance. But something had to be done about Gary.

CHAPTER THIRTY-SIX

A string of multi-colored lights twinkled around the bay window of Karen's row house. Similar lights were strung around the front door where she stood ready to greet her lover, with Coco in her arms. "Gary, I'm so happy you're finally here!" Coco jumped to the floor and scurried away.

The lovers shared a passionate kiss. Karen took him by the hand and led him into her bedroom. "I've missed your touch." They kissed again, and she dropped her robe revealing her nakedness.

"I never get tired of your body." Gary stripped down and threw his clothes on the bed. "Hold that pose and don't start without me," he said, with a crooked smile then kissed her breast. He went into the bathroom and closed the door.

She picked up his clothes to place them on the chaise when his cellphone vibrated in his pant pocket. Karen slipped her hand inside and saw displayed on the screen a photo of Gary and Jane in front of the Vatican, and his home number. A wave of nausea hit her at the sight of the happy couple. "Uh uh . . . he's mine tonight." She turned off the phone and put it back in the pocket.

The bathroom door opened. With the light behind him, Gary stood in the doorway, a naked silhouette.

"Don't just stand there, handsome, I'm waiting."

He walked toward his paramour who lay in a suggestive pose on the bed. He nuzzled her neck and said, "Karen, I hope you understand . . . I can't stay long."

She drew a quick breath. "But while you ARE here, you belong to me." She wrapped her legs tightly around his waist.

Their sex was intense but quick. Gary rolled off her, gathered his clothes, and began to dress.

Karen threw back the covers, jumped out of bed, and jerked her robe off the floor. "Do I at least have time to give you your present or was this just a quick Christmas fuck?"

"I'm sorry, Karen," he said with tenderness. "You know I can't stay long and I'm anxious to give you your gift, too."

She tightened the belt of the robe around her waist, held his hand and walked into the living room.

They sat on the couch, the room illuminated only by the light of the Christmas tree. He removed from his coat pocket a small box wrapped with a silver ribbon and held it out to her. "Karen, I had this made especially for you."

She smiled and unwrapped the box with a childlike eagerness. "This is to die for!" she gushed. She turned on the lamp and held the pendant up to the light. "Oh, Gary. I never expected anything like this!"

"The star in the ruby reminds me of the stars in your eyes," he said, and fastened the chain around her neck.

"Gary, I'll never take it off." Her voice quivered, "You're amazing and to think you had this made just for me." She rubbed her fingers over the crescent shaped moon covered in pavé diamonds and touched the star ruby set in the curve of the pendant.

"It's as unique as you are, Karen."

She leaned toward him and kissed him with fervor. "Now it's my turn." She reached under the tree for his gift. Her hands trembled when she handed him the box adorned with a blue bow.

"You didn't have to get something for me. You're my present." He opened the box. The color drained from his face as he read the lab report.

"I hope it's a boy," Karen said excitedly, and grabbed his hand.

The color drained from Gary's face. "This . . . can't . . . be!"

"I told you I had something special for you." Karen's eyes brimmed with tears. "I thought you'd be happy."

"But you told me you couldn't get pregnant, you were on the pill."

"Darling, I couldn't believe it either."

"This is unacceptable, Karen." He crumpled the paper and threw it to the floor. "You have to do something about it!"

"Do something?" She replied with an astonished look on her face, "I hope you're not suggesting what I think you are! That's not an option."

There was a long silence before Gary spoke. "I can't deal with this right now. I've gotta go." He shooed Coco, who was nestled on his coat, threw it over his arm and walked out, slamming the door behind him.

Karen stood stunned in the middle of the room. "Merry fucking Christmas, Gary!" she cursed, grabbed her glass and threw it at the door.

CHAPTER THIRTY-SEVEN

It was shortly after Ann left that Jane heard the Porsche pull into the garage. The distress on Gary's face was evident when he entered the house. "Gary, what's wrong? Are you alright?" Jane reached up to kiss him but was stopped by his outstretched hand.

"I lost a patient tonight, and no, Jane," Gary barked, "I don't want to discuss it." He tossed his coat over the back of a chair and went to the bar where he poured a generous snifter of brandy, downed a mouthful, then emptied what was left in the decanter into his glass. He turned and glared at Jane, "I thought I told you not to wait up for me."

Jane stiffened. "I called you several times but you didn't answer your phone." She crossed her arms. "Then when I called the hospital you didn't answer your page. I was told you weren't there. I was worried and—"

"You called the hospital?" He looked angry. "What was so damned important that it couldn't wait until I got home?"

"It's not that it was important. You left your wallet here and I just . . . wait a minute, Gary. Since when do I have to get your permission to call you?"

"I don't want my insecure wife calling the hospital for something petty. That's what my cellphone is for."

"Then maybe you should try answering it!"

"Just leave me the hell alone!" Gary threw the snifter. Crystal shards intermingled with brandy sprayed across the floor.

Jane's heart pounded. Her fists tightened. "Gary, why do you have to be so cruel?" She turned her back to him and took several slow, deep breaths. Jane hated the anger she felt and was fearful of losing control. Before she said something she knew she would regret, she left the mess on the floor and walked away. *Your hatefulness has got to stop.*

Jane opened her eyes and felt for Gary's side of the bed. For the third night, she had slept alone. This time, she wouldn't make the first move. If Gary was waiting for her usual apology, he'd have to wait a long time. She hadn't done anything wrong.

CHAPTER THIRTY-EIGHT

Gary looked at his watch and was ready to end his shift when a woman with a broken wrist and a gaping laceration to her head entered the ER. She had tumbled backward into the tub when she was chased into the bathroom by her boyfriend's pot- bellied pig. A homeless man with a self-inflicted knife wound to the hand who claimed to be the messiah was stitched up and admitted to the psyche ward.

Lastly, when a sixty-three-year old man was brought in with a prolapsed rectum, Gary turned that patient over to Dr. Goldberg.

In the doctors' locker room, Gary changed out of his scrubs and prepared to leave when he received a text message. *We have to talk! K.* He returned the text, *Home now. Can't talk.* Before he made his way out of the building, another message came in. *I said, WE NEED TO TALK! K.* His reply, *In bed. Will talk in the a.m.*

Gary walked through the parking lot and neared his vehicle, a movement at the rear of his car startled him.

A figure stepped closer.

Gary reached for car door handle. A hand grabbed his forearm.

"Karen?"

"Really, Gary? Home in bed?"

#

Jane lay awake in bed and rehearsed in her mind what she would say to her husband. As much as she loved him, she was tired of his criticisms and tired of making excuses for his dictatorial conduct. She

161

couldn't accept his hurtfulness toward her any longer. He would have to change, but she knew if she wanted this argument resolved, she'd have to be the one, again, to apologize first. She swore this would be the last time.

Filled with determination, she got out of bed, padded barefoot across the room, and went straight to the guest bedroom to have her talk with Gary. Steam seeped under the bathroom door, the shower was running. The sun had not yet risen and Gary was preparing for work.

Her resolve began to wane. Was she was being too demanding? After all, he had lost a patient this week. Maybe she needed to be more compassionate.

Gary's cellphone pinged. "Gary . . . your phone." He didn't respond. "Gary," she called to him again. Jane picked up the phone to take to him when she glanced at the text message displayed. *I WON'T get an abortion! I want our baby. Tell Jane or I will. K*

Jane stared in disbelief and re-read the message. Her knees buckled. She braced herself against the bed and with an ice-cold hand she returned the phone to the nightstand. Her heart raced. It was difficult to breath. In a daze, her brain a mess of staggered thoughts, she hurried to her room and ran to the bathroom, retching until nothing came up but bile. She sat stunned on the cold marble floor unaware of the passing of time until she heard Gary's car leave the garage.

With both hands on the commode, she pushed herself up and rinsed her mouth at the sink. She pounded the countertop with her fists. "No, Gary, no!" Jane reached for the full bottle of Xanax in the medicine cabinet that Gary prescribed for her anxiety, popped a couple little white pills into her mouth, washed them down with water, then lay on the bed in a fetal position.

#

Through a separation in the drapes, the mid-day sun beamed

across Jane's face which woke her from a deep sleep. She went to the window and opened the drapes wide. A pair of cardinals sang on a branch outside of the window. She heard her housekeeper Leona downstairs singing a Christmas song while she finished her daily chores in the kitchen. It smelled like Leona was baking. *Everything seems so normal.*

"Mrs. Mara," Leona said, as Jane entered the kitchen, "may I make you a cup of coffee?"

Jane nodded to the cheerful woman and tried to clear the cobwebs from her head.

Leona boasted with a wide smile, "I made a pound cake. It's my grandmother's recipe. Can I give you a piece? It's still warm."

Jane saw the look of hopefulness on her housekeeper's face and couldn't say no. "Perhaps a little slice." It was difficult for Jane to swallow the smallest bite but she forced herself to do so. The anguish that gripped her soul made her feel as if the hands of fate had tight fingers around her throat. Regardless, she drank in Leona's gesture of kindness. Leona had worked for them since they moved into this house. She was kind, thoughtful, efficient, and respectful. Jane had grown quite fond of her. If ever there was a time when Jane needed an act of tenderness extended to her, this was the day.

In an emotional fog, Jane wandered through the house, her mind flipped from thought to thought like the chaotic metal orb in a pinball machine. Was 'K' Karen Chapman, the nurse he had the affair with before their trip to Tuscany? Gary swore he ended his relationship with her. Is it my fault because I can't give him a child? Am I going to wake up any minute and find that this was a horrible dream?

"Mrs. Mara, before I leave, is there anything else?" Leona waited. "Mrs. Mara?"

"No, Leona. Thank you." Unaffected by the odd expression on her housekeeper's face, Jane left the room.

#

Alone with her thoughts, Jane sat up rigid on the sofa in the darkened room and stared at the unlit Christmas tree, her half-finished glass of wine on the coffee table. The sun had set, and Jane hadn't bothered to close the drapes. The timer turned on the landscape lighting which cast shadows across the living room walls. Strange, she thought, that while in the middle of her soul searching that she would notice the heater kick on. The soft hum of the furnace took her thoughts back to Millerstown, Ohio—the clang of the old furnace, the unrelenting cold, that horrible winter with Thurman.

In spite of the warmth that filled the room, Jane shivered. The chill she felt came from her soul.

She couldn't shut off her mind and agonized over the text message she'd read, signed 'K.'

I should have seen this coming. Too many times working late; not answering his phone; constant texting, but he's a doctor. Bullshit! He lies about being on-call. He's too tired for sex. Then there's his radical mood swings.

It's the same pattern that I saw before he confessed the first time to having an affair with Karen. I can't un-see the text message.

Still, I love him. What's wrong with me? I must be crazy. I thought I had the perfect life. *My perfect life?*

She couldn't keep torturing herself. She needed answers and she wanted them now. She would confront Gary. Oh hell, what good will it do? He'll only lie. She had her answer. She knew what she had to do.

The sound of Leona's key unlocking the front door awakened Jane.

"Good morning, Mrs. Mara. I'm sorry if I disturbed you."

"Not at all, Leona." Self-conscious of her disheveled appearance and that she was still dressed in the same clothes from yesterday, Jane straightened the pillows on the couch, and went upstairs.

The housekeeper was humming a Christmas carol when Jane returned freshly showered and in clean clothes.

"Leona, I'd like you to take the tree and decorations down today. Dr. Mara and I have decided to go away for New Year's. I know you love these decorations and because I'm changing my theme next year, you're welcome to take all of them with you. When you're done with the tree, please take the rest of the day off. Since we're going to be gone," Jane handed her an envelope, "your check reflects your pay in advance plus a bonus for your loyal service over the years."

"Oh, Mrs. Mara," Leona eyed the check, "you're too generous."

Jane then handed her a small unwrapped box. Leona opened the present that contained the pavé diamond crescent moon with a star ruby.

Filled with melancholy, Jane waited at the front door as Leona's car turned out of the driveway loaded with boxes of Christmas decorations.

CHAPTER THIRTY-NINE

Unable to sleep, Jane laid in her bed lost in a contemplative haze, her mind was filled with jumbled thoughts, none of them made sense. She sat on the edge of the bed. A sudden clarity came to her. She walked to the bathroom and opened the medicine cabinet door wide. She took inventory of the contents on the shelves. Next to the bottle of Xanax was Valium, Zantac, and the Flexeril that Gary had used when he hurt his back at the gym. Emotionless, she studied the medicines and calculated how much would be necessary to obtain the optimal effect.

Startled when she heard Gary enter the bedroom, Jane slammed the cabinet door with such force that the mirror cracked.

"I only came in to get a fresh tie, Jane," he shouted from across the room. "I'll be out of your way in a minute unless you're over your little snit and you want to talk," he reprimanded.

Jane didn't reply.

"For Christ's sake, Jane, get over it. Big deal the hospital told you I wasn't there. But, I was and you're going to have to overcome your ridiculous insecurities."

Jane went into the bedroom, picked up the remote, and turned on the television. The talking head of the weather man indicated heavy rain was expected to last all New Year's Day and may postpone the Mummers Parade.

Gary yelled, "Turn that damned thing off and talk to me, Jane."

She turned up the volume then tramped back to the bathroom and locked the door.

"Dammit Jane, stop being childish." Gary turned off the tv and shouted, "I don't have time for this shit. Grow up and get your head out of your ass before I come home. We're going to settle this to-night!"

Jane heard him curse and slam the bedroom door.

The pitiful face whose vacant eyes looked back at Jane from the broken mirror reflected the emptiness she felt. *She wants their baby!* "You're right, Gary. This will be settled tonight."

The Christmas issue of the hospital bulletin was on the desk where Gary tossed it the night before. Jane turned to a particular page, scribbled something on it, tore out the page and tucked it into her purse. She removed her three-carat diamond engagement ring and slipped it into her pocketbook but left on her plain gold wedding band. She put on a pair of dark sunglasses to conceal her swollen red eyes and left the house.

Her first stop was the bank where in the privacy of the cubicle she emptied their safety deposit box contents into a large manila envelope, folded her engagement ring in the blue handkerchief she carried on her wedding day, and put it inside along with the page she tore from the bulletin, and before she left, had a document notarized. "Step one complete."

At Fed Ex, she placed the oversized envelope and the notarized document inside an overnight mailer and sent it to her sister, Ann. She mentally checked off step two.

On her drive to the hardware store to buy a couple of items, the rain had turned to sleet. Her last stop was the gas station. Jane's car slid slightly up to the pump and almost bumped into a man refueling his car. She waved apologetically at the startled man, swiped her credit card, finished her purchase, and got back inside the car. She looked at the clock in the dashboard. There was plenty of time before Gary was due home.

She sat quietly inside the car in the garage and listened to the whir of the doors close behind her, like this chapter of her life. She took what she bought out of the trunk, made several trips up to the bedroom and concealed the items in the back of the closet. She went into the bathroom to wash her hands that reeked of fuel from the nozzle handle at the service station, opened the medicine cabinet and took a Xanax to calm her nerves. She removed the Flexeril and Valium bottles, shut the cabinet, and stared at the crack in the mirror. The pieces were still together but damaged beyond repair like her marriage.

"Oh Gary, how could you betray me like this?" she sobbed. With tears rolling down her cheeks, she combined most of the pills into one container and dropped that bottle, along with the loose pills, into her pocket, then tossed the empty bottle with Gary's name on the label in the trash can.

Before she headed to the kitchen, Jane stopped at her dresser, opened her jewelry box and fastened around her neck the pearls that Gary had given her as a wedding gift.

Jane stood at the kitchen counter, and with the Onyx pestle clutched tightly in her hand, began to pulverize the white pills into a fine powder. It reminded her of the powdered milk Thurman insisted she would learn to like, to the physical abuse she endured, to the horrific delivery that left her unable to conceive. She hated it when memories of Thurman invaded her thoughts. She never expected to experience that kind of unbearable pain again. *I was foolish to believe your affair with Karen was over.*

Carefully, she emptied the contents from the mortar into the bowl of confectioner's sugar and stirred. She dipped her fingertip into the mixture and tasted it. *Sweet enough.* Once the concoction was complete, she wrapped the empty prescription bottle in paper towels and slammed it into the trash can. "No, you weren't at the hospital, Gary!" she screamed. "You were with your pregnant mistress!"

Jane heard Gary pull into the garage. She waited for him at the kitchen door with the two glasses of brandy she had readied. She smiled at him when he entered.

"Wow, Jane, what's this? I thought you'd still be angry at me."

Jane handed him one of the snifters and said, "Gary, I've thought all day about what you said. I was wrong to be upset over a simple mistake by the hospital. I'm sorry for acting so insecure. I PROMISE it will never happen again." Jane forced a smile and said, "Gary, you'll never know how much I love you." She clinked her glass to his. They drank with their arms entwined and shared a tender kiss.

Gary stepped back and gazed into her eyes, "I'm glad you realize how ridiculous you've been acting." He took a big swig from his snifter. "I really didn't want to have an argument tonight. I'm exhausted and hungry, and I had to drive home in this freezing rain."

"Well, dinner's almost ready." Jane said in a salacious tone, "Why don't we go relax in the living room while you finish your brandy."

"Thanks sweetheart, for the brandy and the apology. I know admitting you're at fault isn't easy for you."

She refreshed his drink. "You know me so well, Gary." Jane lowered her eyes.

Gary took hold of her hand. "Now, that's my good girl." He led Jane into the living room. "What happened to the Christmas tree?" he barked.

"It dried out. I had Leona take it down."

"Hmph. Next year we'll get an artificial tree," he declared.

Gary picked up a match and lit the kindling in the fireplace. They sat together on the sofa and watched the flames dance around the logs. He reached for her hand and placed a light kiss on her palm. "Now that you've said you're going to change, I've decided to try to spend more time at home with you, Jane."

She smiled. "And I've decided I need to serve dinner before it dries out."

Jane wanted everything to be just right. She called to Gary, "Why don't you come here and light the candles?"

It was a romantic dinner they shared by candlelight. Gary was more attentive and complimentary to her than he had been in a long time. At one point, he reached over, stroked her cheek, and told her, 'I love you, Jane. I really do.'

Me, Karen, AND your baby . . . "I know you do, Gary," she pressed his hand to her cheek. "And now for the *pièce de résistance*." Jane scooted her chair away from the table and returned with the platter of apricot crepes covered in 'powdered sugar,' and a crystal bowl filled with more of the sweet, white powder. She put the platter in front of her husband. Jane nibbled on a small plain piece of crepe. Gary spooned more powdered sugar on to his dessert.

"They're good, Jane, but you could have made them sweeter." He ate two more and reached for another which he also generously coated in 'powdered sugar.' Gary wiped his mouth in time to stifle a yawn.

"Gary, am I boring you?" Jane teased.

"No, but I think I've just hit the wall. I'm so-o-o tired and may-be a little drunk," he slurred. "I guess I shouldn't have had the second brandy."

"You mean the third, honey. Gary, you should go to bed. You've had a hard day. I'll be up shortly."

He stood, lost his balance and braced himself against the back of the chair.

Jane hurried to his side. "Let me help you, love." With one hand, she held his arm to steady him, with the other she picked up the brandy decanter from the table. She held on to her husband as he staggered up the stairs and into their bedroom. Gary stumbled onto the bed in a stupor. She removed his shoes, lifted his legs on to the bed, and brushed his hair away from his face as a mother would do to a child.

"Happy New Year, Gary. I love you, forever." She kissed him on his soft, warm mouth.

He didn't respond.

Jane took the decanter of brandy into the bathroom and muttered to herself, "Their baby." She knew she was doing the right thing. Jane swallowed the handful of loose pills that she had in her pocket and washed them down with brandy. She gagged and coughed as the pills scratched her throat.

Once she was certain the pills would stay down, she reached under the sink and grabbed a roll of gauze from the first aid kit. With the skill of a surgical nurse packing a wound, inch by inch she stuffed the gauze into the brandy decanter and left some of the material hanging out from the neck. She placed the bottle on her nightstand. From the drawer, she removed a lighter and their wedding unity candle that had been so lovingly preserved in tissue paper. She set them down next to the bottle. Jane went to the bedroom closet where she had stored the red gas cans filled with diesel fuel that she had purchased that afternoon. She soaked the carpet in front of the bedroom doors and windows with the liquid. What was left in the can was poured on the marble bathroom floor. *Block all exits.* The second can of diesel fuel she splashed around the bed and over the rest of the carpet.

Jane's eyes stung from the fumes. Mucous flowed from her nose. Her chest burned.

She stood next to the bed, her husband remained unconscious. He had not moved since she tucked him in. His breathing was shallow. *Tell Jane or I will . . .* The thought of Gary with Karen was unbearable. Jane leaned over Gary and whispered in his ear, "I will love you through eternity," and kissed him.

She would have to move quickly. She could feel the effects of Xanax and Flexeril that had started to kick in. Jane removed the .38 caliber revolver from Gary's drawer and pressed the barrel of the gun to the middle of his chest. "This is the only way." She squeezed the trigger. Her ears rang, her head pounded. She tossed the gun on her side of the bed.

Jane removed her precious copy of <u>Gone With The Wind</u> from her nightstand, laid it on the comforter, and with arms and legs that she struggled to control, climbed on to the bed. The pills and brandy had kicked in. She was whoozie and knew she was about to lose consciousness.

She picked up the Unity candle that felt heavy in her weakened grip and fumbled with the lighter to ignite the wick. With an unsteady hand, she set the lit candle precariously on the edge of the nightstand. In a fugue state, she was vaguely aware of lighting the gauze in the brandy bottle off the flame of the candle and tossing the Molotov cocktail across the room. Through half-closed eyes, she saw the blaze. Her semi-conscious mind didn't register danger or fear.

With her outstretched hand, she touched her cherished book and drew it to her heart then felt for the gun. As Jane lost consciousness, she mumbled, "Ashes to ashes."

Flames engulfed the room. Rancid smoke had suffocated the life from Jane. The slow burning diesel accelerant burned with such intensity that the bodies were destroyed beyond recognition.

CHAPTER FORTY

Ann woke early New Year's morning with an ominous feeling as if she'd had a terrible nightmare—one she couldn't recall. She put on her robe and went directly to the kitchen to start the coffee. Her apartment felt as chilled as the ice-covered trees across the street. She turned up the heat and drew her robe more tightly around her. Although warm air blew from the register, dread gripped her heart with ice cold fingers. Whatever the nightmare had been, she couldn't shake the remnants of the dream that left her with the sense of foreboding.

Ann took a steamy shower and hoped the hot water would wash away the energy of the bad dream. She stood under the spray until it became tepid. The shower did little to alleviate her angst.

She started to dress and began to cough so hard she was unable to catch her breath. Forced to sit on the bed to steady herself, she took a big gulp of air and filled her lungs. Once the episode subsided, "God, I hate this rotten cold weather. I refuse to get sick!"

Dressed in her woolen slacks and turtleneck sweater, Ann went to the kitchen cabinet, opened the bottle of vitamin C, and took a couple tablets with a glass of orange juice. She poured herself a cup of coffee and went to the front door to get the newspaper.

"Happy New Year!" Mrs. Bolinski shouted to a couple at the far end of the hall. Ann tried to ignore her annoying neighbor, but it was too late.

"Oh, Ms. Paxton, Happy New Year to you, too!" Mrs. Bolinski's screech echoed down the hallway.

173

Ann gave a disinterested wave, picked up the paper and stepped back into her condo.

Relaxed on her over-stuffed sofa, the effects of the nightmare dissipated, Ann settled in to read the newspaper. The frontpage headline read: Freezing Rain Forces the Mummer's Parade to be Rescheduled. The bottom half of the page was filled with a photograph of a six-car pile-up on the expressway attributed to the ice storm.

She opened the paper and read the caption: Fatal House Fire on the Main Line. Arson Suspected. Ann immediately recognized in the foreground of a photograph, the distinctive mailbox that was a replica of Jane's Georgian home. In the photograph, firetrucks were on the street and firemen stood on the lawn.

Ann jumped to her feet. Her hands clenched the paper as she read that the home belonged to a prominent University Hospital physician, Dr. Gary Mara and his wife. Two bodies were found inside the charred structure. Positive identification is pending.

Ann dropped the paper as her knees buckled and she collapsed to the floor. She grasped the collar of her robe, curled up in anguish and began to wail.

Mrs. Bolinski's incessant banging on the door snapped Ann out of her shock.

"Ms. Paxton, Ms. Paxton, are you alright?" There were several more bangs at the door. "Ms. Paxton, should I go for help?"

"No, no." Ann forced herself to take a breath, "I'm fine."

"You don't sound fine. I'd feel better if you let me come in."

"Please . . . I'm okay," Ann insisted. "I dropped a pot of hot water on the floor and on my slippers. I'm cleaning up the mess now. Please, just go away."

Ann didn't need to wait for the pending identification of the bodies found in the house. She knew they were Jane and Gary, but she desperately wanted to be wrong. Ann texted, emailed, and phoned them, to no avail. The police gave her no information because she couldn't prove she was a relative. As a last resort, Ann called the hospital and asked for Dr. Mara. She was told no information could be given on Dr. Mara.

#

The stack of files Michael brought home from the office to review over the holiday weekend, kept him up late. He drifted off surrounded by work. He was in a deep sleep when an early morning call woke him. He reached for the phone and knocked the Browning file he had worked on before he fell asleep, off the bed. The contents spilled on to the floor. "Aw shit!"

He checked the caller ID, cleared his throat, and answered, "Good morning, Meg. Happy New Year!"

"Not so happy. We'll have to cancel our dinner tonight. Something terrible has happened. The department is upside down right now."

"Are you alright, Meg?" She sounded like she was on the verge of tears.

"I'm okay but pretty shaken. One of our doctors, Dr. Mara—you remember, he fixed your hand in the E.R. the day we met—he and his wife died last night when their house caught fire."

"My God, Meg, how did it happen?"

"We don't know the details yet, but everyone is extremely upset." Meg went on to explain that Dr. Mara's nurse, Karen, showed up for her shift and became hysterical and collapsed when she heard the news. "One of the hospital volunteers had to drive her home. I have to cover Karen's shift and I won't be done until late."

Michael propped himself up on the pillow. "Don't worry about our dinner. Right now, I'm more concerned about you."

"Really, I'm okay, Michael. But, I can't stop thinking that I just worked with Dr. Mara a couple days ago. Everyone loved him. I spent a lot of time with his wife on the hospital charity board. I didn't know her well because she quit right after I joined, but she was always so nice. I know this is a cliché, Michael, but you never think something like this will happen to someone you know. It's such a shock."

"Meg, is there anything I can do? Do you want to come here after your shift? I'll cook dinner for you."

"That sounds perfect. Michael. Let's promise not to take each other for granted and never let a day go by that we don't say, 'I love you.'"

Michael thought about the conversation he had with Meg. She was right. He'd never let a day go by without telling her how much he loved her.

Unable to fall back to sleep, Michael stood, stretched and groaned. He smiled as he remembered the first time Meg stayed over and witnessed his morning stretch. She said he reminded her of a grizzly bear waking from hibernation.

Michael's New Year's resolution was to finish the paperwork on several cases including the Browning case from which he had been fired. He reached down to pick up the mess that had scattered on the floor. Mixed in with the papers was the composite drawing of Trey Browning's assailant. Michael studied the sketch. There was something that nagged at him, something he couldn't put his finger on, something . . .

When he wore a badge in Tampa, Michael worked on a case until it was resolved or went cold. He found the biggest adjustment he had to make when he became a P.I. was to close the books in the middle of a case when he was ordered to do so, as with Mr. Browning.

CHAPTER FORTY-ONE

Sleep evaded Ann. No matter how hard she tried, she couldn't control her thoughts as they swirled in her mind like a cyclone in her head—memories of sweet, sweet, Jane. She remembered them as children and how Jane would listen with attentiveness as she read aloud to her. Ann knew Jane didn't understand most of the story of the old south, but she loved Jane's giggles and questions about the story. She thought about the day their foster-mother dressed the two of them in matching blue, Dotted Swiss dresses and how excited they were that people would think they were real sisters. Ann relived the day she pushed 'Uncle Johnny' down the cellar steps and how happy she and Jane were when the ambulance hauled his body away. That monster would never be able to hurt them again.

Ann lay in bed, her eyes focused on the clock. Minutes passed like hours. Ann wanted to believe that Jane died of smoke inhalation before the fire consumed her. Emotionally paralyzed, Ann's body was as numb as her mind. She'd never felt powerless, until now.

Desperate for sleep, Ann took a sleeping pill and closed her eyes.

Smoke, flames, coughing, running to the ringing phone. Jane, I'm here, I'm coming... Ring, ring, ring. Don't hang up. I'm coming. Where are you? Where's the phone? Smoke, flames. Ring, ring, ring.

More asleep than awake, she reached for her phone. "Jane?"

"Happy New Year, Ms. Paxton. This is your concierge, Hilmer," he said, with a cheerful voice. "I have a package here for you—"

"This is not a good time." She started to hang up, "I'll get it later."

"I do apologize, Ms. Paxton. But the package is marked 'urgent' in big letters. I thought you should know."

Ann sat up and rubbed her eyes. Not caring to hide her annoyance, she asked, "Who is it from, Hilmer?"

"Let me see . . . Oh, I'll have to get my glasses. My arms aren't as long as they use to be." He chuckled. "Yes, I see it now. It's from a Mrs. Jane Mara."

Ann caught her breath. "Send it up immediately," she demanded.

Braced with her back against her closed front door, Ann clutched the package to her chest. The only sound she heard was her pulse pounding in her head. With a robotic gait, Ann made her way to the sofa, opened the package and emptied the contents on to the glass top table.

The clink of her sister's diamond engagement ring hitting the glass echoed in her ears. It all seemed surreal. Ann reached for the ring and held it in her palm for several minutes then slipped it on her trembling hand.

A notarized statement was on top of the papers in front of Ann. It gave her instructions and authority to disperse Jane's valuable stocks and Bearer bonds, that were included in the package, to women's shelters in Philadelphia.

An envelope included with the documents Ann recognized as one from Jane's monogrammed stationary. She withdrew the handwritten note and read:

> *Dearest Ann,*
> *My heart is broken because I know how much my actions have hurt you.*
> *For that I am so sorry.*
> *Ann, when I was a teenager I was pregnant and in an extremely abusive relationship. Because of that, my baby girl, Scarlett, died and I could no longer have children. I suffered more pain than I thought was humanly possible. But I sur-*

vived. I started a new life. Years later, Fate brought you back to me and I was happy.

And now I have discovered Gary's infidelity and that his mistress, Karen Chapman, is pregnant. My pain is beyond endurance.

Please forgive me. I love you forever. Jane

"If I told you what I knew about Gary, I could have helped you through it and you'd still be here." Ann surrendered her control and cried without restraint.

It was hours later before she was composed enough to sort through the stocks and bonds. In the package, Ann found a page that appeared to be torn from a magazine. On it a photograph pictured a group of men and women, some wearing Santa hats and others who held mistletoe over their head. A circle was drawn around the face of a pretty dark-haired woman. In the caption under the picture, the name Karen Chapman was double-underlined.

CHAPTER FORTY-TWO

The procession of cars drove under the wrought iron arch of the snow-covered cemetery. The silver hearse that carried the casket of Gary Mara wound its way through the old graveyard past large monuments and stone mausoleums. It was followed by a long line of vehicles that came to a stop behind the hearse when it arrived at its destination. An artificial grass runner had been laid on the snow-cleared path to create a walkway that lead up to the gravesite. His elderly parents got out of the first limousine and made their way up the runner. They had learned from a detective on the scene that their son was the victim of an alleged murder/suicide.

Michael opened the door for Meg and noticed a dark blue Lexus parked facing the wrong way on the narrow one-way drive. A sudden gust of frigid air whipped Meg's scarf from around her neck and blew it in the direction of the blue car. Michael took off after it and saw a woman inside the Lexus. At first glance, it looked like she was using opera glasses to scan the crowd. Michael caught site of the scarf as it landed in the snow and scooped it off the ground. He turned around and saw the woman in the car quickly turned her head away from him.

He returned to Meg who shivered as he wrapped the scarf around her neck. The brutal January wind matched the solemn mood of the day.

"I'm glad you're here with me, Michael." Meg held onto his arm as they made their way to join the other mourners at the gravesite. "It looks like a lot of hospital staff is here," she said. "I even recognize a few patients."

The service had begun when Michael noticed out of the corner of his eye, the woman from the Lexus walk up and stand behind the crowd. She scanned the faces in the group and seemed to focus on someone across from her like a cat stalking a canary. He was transfixed by the odd sense of hostility that emanated from the woman.

Meg tugged at Michael's sleeve and whispered, "What are you looking at?"

"That woman standing behind everyone; do you know who she is?"

"I have no idea," she answered.

"What about that brunette over there?" Michael nodded to a woman who sat in the last row of white chairs behind the family. ". . . the woman crying—in the light brown coat."

Meg explained that she was Dr. Mara's nurse, Karen Chapman. "Why do you ask?"

"Just curious," Michael said, and gently squeezed her hand.

Before the casket was lowered and the service concluded, Michael saw the woman from the Lexus leave the group and walk toward her car. She had had no interaction with anyone that he noticed. There was nothing that she had done that was out of the ordinary, yet, there was something about her that didn't feel right.

The crowd dispersed after the final prayer. Meg introduced Michael to several co-workers who approached her, that included Karen Chapman. They commiserated about the terrible loss and spoke of their fond memories of Dr. Mara. Karen waited for the others to walk away then hugged Meg and broke down.

"I'm so lost," Karen cried. "I can't imagine my life without him. What do I do now?"

Meg looked perplexed.

"The police said it was a murder/suicide." Karen sobbed, "If she was so damn miserable, why didn't she just kill herself? Why did she have to kill him too?"

Meg gasped and took a step back.

"I'm sorry, Meg," Karen used her gloved hand to wipe away tears. "That comment was uncalled for."

Karen's emotional outburst made Michael suspect that there was more to her relationship with Dr. Mara. He knew hospital affairs were as common as in the cop shops.

Michael turned around to give the two women private time and caught the woman inside the Lexus staring in their direction. Her hostile glare fixed on Meg and Karen. You didn't have to be a detective to know that something wasn't kosher.

Michael excused himself from Karen and Meg on the pretext that he needed his hat. He walked by the Lexus and made a mental note of the license number. He went to his car and jotted down the plate information on a piece of paper he took from the center console. From his position, Michael saw Meg take a subtle peek over her shoulder, an obvious look of discomfort on her face, and thought she needed a 'rescue.' When he rejoined them, Meg took the cue and said a hasty goodbye to Karen.

Neither of them spoke until Karen was out of ear shot. Michael said, "I hope you don't think I'm insensitive—"

"You're not, and I thank you." Meg kissed his cheek. "That conversation was quite awkward." She tucked her arm under his and said, "Let's get out of here, I'm freezing."

They sat inside his car until the heater warmed. "Michael," Meg sighed, "there's been talk at the hospital that Karen and Dr. Mara had been having an affair for a long time, but I don't pay much attention to gossip. After what I just heard from her, I think the rumors were true. I'm shocked that Karen just opened up to me like that. We've never been more than co-workers."

"It was kind of you to let her vent, Meg. I could tell she was really upset."

"Karen said she hated to go back to work. She said everyone is whispering behind her back, as if she had some fault in what happened."

"Meg, if the rumors are true then maybe she did."

Michael put the car in gear and took notice that most of the people had left the grounds, but Karen's SUV and the blue Lexus were in front of him. He saw the Lexus make a quick U-turn and exit out of the cemetery behind Karen's SUV.

#

The sky was gray and bleak. The temperature had plummeted. Ice formed on the road. Karen Chapman's vehicle fishtailed as she made a left turn out of the cemetery and onto the street. Ann allowed another car to pass before she pulled in the line of traffic and headed in the same direction as Karen. It wasn't long before Karen stopped at the curb in front of a brick rowhouse, climbed the white marble steps of the home, and entered.

Ann kept a watchful eye on the brunette during the funeral service to make sure this was the woman from Jane's note. Ann had no doubt that Karen Chapman was not pregnant and had never been pregnant.

Jane had died for a lie.

Over the next few weeks, Ann stalked Karen. Every morning she left the rowhouse bundled in her winter coat and scarf and headed to the cemetery. She'd stay for a short while at his grave then drive to the hospital. After her shift, Karen drove home with an occasional stop at the grocer's, dry cleaners, or gas station. Once at home, she'd stay in until the next morning. Ann never witnessed any visitors to the home. There was only that stupid white cat who sat in the window.

Confident that she knew Karen's routine, Ann began to plot the Divine Justice that Karen would come to know. "You destroyed my family and you will pay." No one would be able to connect Ann to Karen's death; a death that would look like death by fire.

#

A small cardboard box filled with the cremains of Jane Mara sat on a metal shelf in the backroom of the crematorium.

There would be no procession of cars under the wrought iron arch, nor a silver hearse to carry the remains of Jane Mara to her final resting place. There was only a cold, dark room in the coroner's office filled with cardboard boxes that contained unclaimed cremains.

CHAPTER FORTY-THREE

The early morning light shone into Michael's office as he sorted through the stack of files on his desk. Sylvie left the paperwork for him to complete over the weekend. As he grabbed the next file he recognized the next name on the file. It was the Anne Preston/Ann Paxton folder, the job that his brother George had completed. Michael scanned the itemized list of purchases his brother had made during his assignment and shook his head and snickered as he pictured his brother wearing a red woolen Santa cap as a disguise while he tailed Ann Paxton.

There were too many similarities between Preston/Paxton to sweep under the rug, yet there was no hard evidence to support that they were the same person. He understood Allison's disappointment when he reported nothing suspicious was found during the Ann Paxton surveillance. He'd promised Allison he'd keep looking, and he would.

Michael made a notation inside the folder for Sylvie; No charge to Allison Rogers DeMarcou.

From under the papers in the Preston/Paxton file, the corner of a photograph was visible. It was the enlarged Driver's License picture of Ann Paxton. He'd looked at it a hundred times . . . *I'll be damned.*

"SYLVIE! Bring me the Browning file, asap!"

He placed Ann's Driver's License picture side-by-side with the composite drawing of Trey Browning's attacker. "I'll be a son-of-a-bitch!"

He dialed Trey Browning's number and paced the room while he waited for him to answer.

"Ron Browning here."

Caught off guard when his father answered Trey's phone, "Mr. Browning, this is Michael Vega. I need to talk to Trey."

"Well you can't. You're gonna have to talk to me. What the hell do you want, anyway? I fired you."

"I may have identified his assailant, Mr. Browning."

"Yeah, I've heard that before from everybody else I hired, and the cops. Nothing has panned out. So, you'd better not be fucking with me. If you're just trying to get more money out of me, Vega, you can go fuck yourself."

Michael's jaw tightened. "Mr. Browning, I have a picture I need to show Trey."

"Vega, you'd better not be playin' me."

"Mr. Browning, I don't have time to play games. You don't want Trey to see the picture, I'll take it to the police."

". . . Alright, Vega, but you'll have to come here. He's not up to leaving the house. And if you're right, you'll get paid for your time."

CHAPTER FORTY-FOUR

It was late afternoon when Michael approached the Browning estate. He was amused to see that the man's ego was reflected in the giant brass 'B' that topped the ornate black gate. He spoke into the callbox and was buzzed in by Ron Browning. Michael drove up the long, paved driveway and was impressed by the six-car garage attached to the house. He envisioned it filled with big ass luxury cars, a reflection of Browning's inflated sense of importance.

Michael parked on the driveway between a pair of ostentatious bronze lions and was met at the front door by an attractive buxom middle-aged woman in a maid's uniform.

"You must be Detective Vega." she said.

"No. I'm Michael Vega, a private investigator not a cop."

"Oh yes. Mr. Browning is expecting you," and promptly ushered him to the den. The ten-foot-high double doors were opened into a room that smelled of new leather. The furniture looked as though it had never been sat upon. The pristine space appeared staged for a photo shoot in the Dupont Registry. Library shelves were lined with leather bound books that Michael assumed Browning had never read. The scant personal affects in the room were those of Ron Browning's football trophies. Michael thought it odd that there were no family pictures nor awards represented for his superstar son. He suspected this space was more of a showroom for the megalomaniac father.

At the sound of footsteps, Michael turned to see Browning enter the room in front of, who Michael assumed was, his son. From his father's description, Michael never would have recognized Trey. The young man who extended his hand to Michael was gaunt and pale, and half the size of what he appeared to be in the pictures his father had shown Michael at their first meeting. Michael doubted Trey could walk onto a football field let alone play a game.

Trey's manner was subdued. "Mr. Vega, my father said—"

"Trey let me handle this," Browning interrupted. "You said you had something for my boy to look at."

Of course, Browning would try to monopolize the meeting. Michael turned and spoke to the young man. "Trey, before I show this to you," Michael held up a piece of paper, "can you tell me what you remember about the woman who attacked you? Can you describe her again?"

"I'll never forget—"

"Show him the damn picture, Vega."

"Dad, please. I've got this." Trey's forehead creased, and he swallowed hard. "The one thing I will never forget are her eyes. I've never seen eyes that green—and, her long red hair." He described what she wore that night and said she was built like a cheerleader.

"Was she that young?" Michael asked, aware of Trey's initial report of the woman being in her forties.

"No, she was older, more like a cheerleader's mother." He added, "I remember she was little and didn't weigh more than a buck and a quarter."

"What about moles, scars, tattoos, any marks at all?"

"None that I saw."

"Do you think you would recognize her if you saw her again?"

"Damn straight I would. Wouldn't you remember the psycho who cut off your balls?" Trey tensed. His angry eyes filled with tears. "I'll never forget that face."

Michael handed the enlarged picture taken from Ann's driver's license to the young man.

The second Trey saw the likeness, his eyes widened, and he shrieked, "Holy shit! That's her!" Tears streamed down his face. "The hair is different but that's her. I'm a thousand percent sure." He choked, "That's her."

Browning grabbed the paper from his son's trembling hand. "Where the hell is she? How did you find her? Does she know you're on to her?" Browning machine-gunned Michael with questions. "Tell me where I can find her. I'm gonna take care of this myself." His blood-red face seethed with anger.

As much as Michael despised Ron Browning, he could understand the father's frustration at Trey's assailant not being caught, but Michael wouldn't condone what Browning wanted to do.

"Don't give me that condescending look, Vega. Tell me where I can find her. I'll give you whatever you want. Name your price." Browning's persona filled with murderous intent.

"You know that's never going to happen, Mr. Browning." Michael took the paper with Ann Paxton's photo on it from the man and put it in his briefcase. "I have to turn this over to the police. They'll take care of it."

"Vega, can't we work this out?" He bargained, "I won't implicate you." Browning's voice was controlled but on the verge of rage. "I already told you I'll pay you whatever you want."

Insulted by Browning's repeated offers to buy him off, Michael shot a look of disgust at the father, turned toward Trey and handed him his card. "If you think of anything else, give me a call."

Michael glared at the father. "Don't get up, I'll let myself out."

On the drive back to the city, Michael called Detective Rizzo, Connor's buddy at the Philadelphia Police Department who gave him the copy of Paxton's driver's license when Michael told him he was working on a cold case. The favor of giving Michael the information was not illegal, but it certainly was in the gray area since Michael was no longer a law enforcement officer. The detective could have received a severe reprimand. For that reason, Michael would only speak with Rizzo and give him the positive identification from Trey Browning of his assailant.

He left a voice message for Rizzo to call ASAP.

The off-ramp for the expressway Service Center was up ahead. Michael was hungry and wanted to stop for a Nathan's hot dog. He was next up to the counter when his cellphone rang. 'Private Caller' showed on the screen. Michael stepped out of line to take the call.

"Vega."

"I need to talk to you."

It was Trey's voice he heard and not Detective Rizzo's. Michael heard a lot of commotion in the background, he asked, "What's going on?"

"My father's out of control. He's in the other room smashing things. Can you hear that? He's yelling about the woman. He wants to kill her. He's screaming at my mother and she's crying. He says I'll never play football again. I'll never be a real man." Trey's voice cracked. "What good am I? I'll never be the man my father expected me to be."

There was the sound of breaking glass and a man wailing in the distance, "My son's a goddamn eunuch." Michael was astonished. What he heard was incomprehensible. "Trey, I'm sure he didn't mean that." Michael heard a muffled sob. "Trey, are you there? Trey? Trey?"

BANG!

"Oh, GOD!" Patrons who waited in line at the Nathan's counter, gawked at Michael. "Trey? Trey?" Michael disconnected the call and dialed the Browning's home phone, his hand shook. The line was busy. He dialed again and again. Michael was ready to call 9-1-1 but tried the house one last time. The maid answered.

"B-B-Browning residence."

"This is Michael Vega. I was just there. I need to speak with Mr. Browning, right now!"

"He can't come to the phone. There's been a terrible accident." The woman broke down and became hysterical. "Oh, Mr. Vega, he's dead! He's dead! Oh my God, Trey's dead!"

Over the sound of her crying, Michael heard sirens. He hung up, re-dialed Detective Rizzo and left an urgent message.

#

Sweaty from his morning jog, Michael was ready to jump in the shower when Rizzo called.

"Hey, thanks for getting back to me. I got a hit on that driver's license. The victim of an attack made a positive I.D. of the assailant." Michael filled him in on the particulars of the Browning case.

"Yeah, I heard about that. That's the guy who got his nut sack flushed. Vega, thanks for the info. I'll pass it on to the Jersey state police. They'll need to talk to the victim."

"That's going to be tough. The kid off'd himself yesterday."

"No shit?" Rizzo huffed, "Well that's Jersey's problem now."

The conversation took a different direction as Michael explained the link between the woman in the driver's license photo— Ann Paxton, a.k.a. Anne Preston, and a serial killer case in Florida.

"Damn Vega, next you're going to tell me you found Jimmy Hoffa," Rizzo laughed. "If this information pans out, you're going to make me look damn good. If it doesn't, you'll owe me a beer . . . or two . . . make that a whole damn case."

"You got it, buddy."

"Thanks for the Browning info, Vega. Go ahead and send me what you have on the Florida case and I'll make some calls. I'll get back to you when I have something."

Michael thought about calling Allison but reconsidered. He'd wait until Rizzo gave him confirmation—either way.

CHAPTER FORTY-FIVE

Ann walked the three short blocks from her office on Walnut Street to the building where Seymour Bradley, Esquire had his family law practice. Dressed in an overcoat that covered a dark woolen suit and carrying a stylish briefcase, Ann could have easily been mistaken for an attorney on her way to court. Inside the austere lobby, she checked the directory and found the location of Mr. Bradley's suite.

The polished mahogany interior of the elevator filled to capacity with a herd of people who reminded Ann of cattle dressed in business suits. They stared straight ahead at the shiny metal doors like animals who waited for the pen to open . . . *fillers*, people occupying space, breathing in and out, just existing. She looked at them with disdain.

On the third floor, several people exited, and an older woman entered the lift wearing an abundance of Wind Song perfume. Florence, the foster-mother that Ann and Jane had so loved always wore that fragrance. In an instant, Ann was lost in her memories of the gentle woman who taught them so much. She recalled how Jane responded to the smallest act of encouragement and flourished under Florence's kindness. *Would she want to know about Jane's death? No. Why hurt her too?*

The mature 'Wind Song' woman and Ann got out on the same floor and walked into the attorney's outer office. The lady stepped in front of Ann, handed papers to the perky receptionist and said, "Mr. Bradley is expecting these." The woman turned to leave and smiled.

The receptionist then acknowledged Ann. "Ms. Paxton?"

Ann nodded.

"Mr. Bradley will be with you shortly."

Ann seated herself across the room, remnants of childhood memories lingered, stirred by the scent of the woman's perfume. A stark piece of art on the wall caught her attention. It was a Colombo watercolor of an old rusted out truck in the middle of a field, titled, 'Abandoned.' How apropos. *I am . . . without Jane.*

It was a short wait before she was escorted into an elegant conference room and greeted by an amenable man who appeared to be in his seventies. He introduced himself as Seymour Bradley.

He extended his hand and told her how very sorry he was for her loss. "I knew Jane for as long as she lived in Philadelphia. She was an incredible woman, the epitome of generosity. What a tragedy." The man dabbed a tear with a monogrammed handkerchief and gestured for Ann to be seated.

She felt his sincerity was genuine.

Ann spoke in a soft, controlled voice, "Mr. Bradley, as I told you over the phone, I'd like to have Jane's last wishes put into place as soon as possible." She handed him papers from the briefcase minus the handwritten note describing Gary's betrayal with Karen Chapman.

"As you can see, Mr. Bradley, it was important to Jane that this woman's shelter be named Scarlett's House." The notarized instructions Jane had left clearly stated her wishes.

He nodded and began to leaf through the paperwork. Ann sensed that he was aware of the significance of the name Scarlett and understood why Jane insisted that he be the lawyer to execute her requests. He emanated an energy of caring and trust.

Mr. Bradley glanced at her quizzically with a hint of a smile.

Ann realized that he saw her staring at him.

He spoke first, "Ms. Paxton, I will call you as soon as these documents are ready for you to sign."

Ann rose to leave. "Thank you. I will wait for your call."

He walked her to the door and placed a gentle touch on her shoulder. "This is a wonderful legacy from Jane that will improve the lives of many women and children."

As Ann passed through the lobby, she stopped in front of the watercolor. *Jane, thanks to you, the people at Scarlett's House won't be abandoned.*

On the walk back to her office, she stopped at a corner luncheonette for a hot cup of soup and a bite to eat. She had taken her first spoonful of chili when she heard a familiar voice from the booth behind her.

"Ms. Paxton, I thought that was you. Oh, what a coincidence. We're both having chili. Is it okay if I join you?" Donna Lobianco, the girl who Ann counseled after Trey Browning raped her, didn't wait for Ann's response, picked up her bowl, and seated herself across from Ann.

"Well, I was just finishing, but if you insist . . ."

"Mom's at the hairdresser next door and I hate to eat alone. I'm so glad I saw you." Donna waved to the waitress to bring the rest of her ample lunch order to that booth, apparently oblivious at Ann's annoyance at her intrusion.

"It's so nice that we can have lunch together." Donna was all smiles. "I don't know how I can thank you enough for how you helped me through my horrible ordeal. At first, I didn't believe you when you said that I would be okay. But you were right. I started in therapy and it really helps." The girl hesitated before she asked, "Ms. Paxton, what do you see for my future now?"

"Donna, I never read anyone outside of my office." Ann bristled, "If you're anxious to know something, you can call me for an appointment."

"Oh, okay," Donna sounded a little disappointed.

Mrs. Lobianco approached the booth sporting her freshly styled, over-teased hair. "My goodness, look at you two!"

Ann was astonished as Mrs. Lobianco slid into the booth alongside Donna and got comfortable.

"Ms. Paxton, I guess Donna's been talking your ear off about Trey Browning. I heard he blew his head off right in front of his parents." Mrs. Lobianco took the spoon from her daughter's hand, scooped chili from the bowl, shoved it into her mouth, and continued to speak. "I wish he'd have done it sooner. A lot of gullible young women wouldn't have suffered." Mrs. Lobianco tilted her head, and said, "I suppose I should feel sorry for his parents, but I don't. My compassion is for the girls he raped."

Ann replied, "But it IS a tragedy for his family."

Mrs. Lobianco opened a packet of crackers and crumbled them into her daughter's bowl of chili. "Well, speaking of his family, maybe if they had raised him right, he wouldn't have turned out to be such a monster. If you can keep a secret, my hairdresser made me promise not to say anything but . . . one of her customers is an EMT who responded to the Browning house when it happened and overheard someone say that right before he killed himself, a detective came to the house with information about the identification of the woman who cut off his balls."

The hairs on the back of Ann's neck stood up, her heart pounded. "I guarantee I won't repeat what you told me." She placed money on the table, bid the women a good afternoon, and made an abrupt exit.

Outside, she took a deep breath. She had to think.

CHAPTER FORTY-SIX

The office that Ann had so carefully selected on Walnut Street was now as dismal, cold, and dark as her entire being felt. She emptied the safe and left the door wide open. With a heavy sigh, she perused the room and took in what remained to be done. She cleared out the contents of her desk drawer, placed her scant personal belongings inside her briefcase, and deposited her hot pink stun gun in her purse. The Lalique clock that once represented the potential financial success she could obtain in her real identity as Ann Paxton, now reminded her of all that she had lost. She rejected the idea to take it with her.

Ann slammed the office door shut. The pulse in her neck throbbed as she walked away.

Outside on the pavement, Ann cursed under her breath. She had been diligent in structuring her rebirth in Philadelphia. Her intention to forget her past and start an uncomplicated new life had been successful until the powerful draw to the necessity of her *mission* caught up with her. It all started again with the perverted plumber, James Bakker who had to pay for what he did to his innocent niece. Then came Judge Carroll, the bastard who punished a pedophile with little more than a slap on the wrist. They each thought they had gotten away with their crimes until she balanced the scales of justice.

Would she ever be able to change her destiny that began when she was a child and she protected Jane from 'Uncle Johnny'? Ann closed her eyes and relived the satisfaction she felt when she killed him. That's when she knew she was meant to be the hand of karma.

She regretted not killing Trey Browning at the motel and made a silent vow never to let another monster live with his deformity as a punishment. So much for mercy. That mistake left her vulnerable. The risk of discovery was imminent. She was being forced to leave.

There was one remaining obligation to complete.

Driven by a festering hatred, Ann strategized the details of her plan to make Karen suffer for the affair she had with Gary, for ruining her sister's marriage, and for the pain she caused sweet, sweet, Jane. That whore will beg for death for what she forced Jane to do.

There would be no mercy.

Ann's blood ran cold with bitterness at the thought of exacting karma on Karen.

CHAPTER FORTY-SEVEN

The receptionist escorted Ann into Mr. Bradley's conference room. He entered smiling like a Cheshire cat, greeted Ann and said, "Jane must have used her heavenly influence to help me process all of this paperwork without a glitch. It doesn't usually happen this fast," he boasted.

"How perceptive of you, Mr. Bradley. I have no doubt that Jane is working her magic."

"From Heaven, I'm certain," he said, and patted her hand. Mr. Bradley called in the receptionist to witness and notarize the papers Ann was signing. "Ms. Paxton, I believe this will take care of everything."

Not quite, Mr. Bradley.

He escorted Ann through the office and said, "If there is anything else I can do for you, and of course for Jane, please don't hesitate to call."

"Thank you, Mr. Bradley." *The rest I'll do on my own.*

Confident that every detail of her plan was coming to fruition, Ann walked through the lobby of the office building surrounded by the morning hustle and bustle of the insignificant 'worker bees.' Ann considered them little more than hamsters on a wheel, going 'round and 'round. She knew that none of these self-absorbed lemmings would make the sacrifices she had to protect the innocent.

Ann turned up the collar of her coat, slipped on her gloves and noticed the bald maintenance man with rheumy eyes, dressed in a tattered Army surplus overcoat, sweep the steps in front of the building. The man nodded and mumbled a pleasant 'mornin' as she walked past. Ann intuitively sensed that he too was once one of the hamsters on the wheel but chose to jump off and leave the scratch-ing-his-way-to-the-top, behind.

She hailed the first cab that she saw and instructed the driver to take her to the mechanic's garage that belonged to the man she spoke with from Craig's List. Within the hour, she had paid a thousand dollars cash for an old white Chevy Malibu. She cranked the heat to maximum and lowered the windows to air-out the musty odor. The bitter cold air was preferable to the smell. The old beater would have to do to get her out of town fast and under the radar as soon as she took care of Karen. She'd replace it with a more suitable vehicle when she arrived at her new destination.

On a narrow side street in the middle of a clean but modest neighborhood, Ann got out of the car and locked the door. Twice she walked the distance from where she left the junker to the lot where she would lure Karen. She gauged that the walk would take no longer than four minutes to return to the Malibu after Karen's karma was complete.

"Oh, great." It started to snow.

Ann draped her scarf over her head and walked hurriedly up the sidewalk through the neighborhood of rowhouses that were the same as every other block, red brick with white marble steps. Ann noticed that the front door of each house was different. Some were painted vibrant colors, others were more ornate, and one door she passed had a stained glass insert. She smirked at their desperate and piteous attempt at individuality.

"Damn, damn, damn!" she blurted as she tripped on the uneven brick sidewalk, caught herself on a fire hydrant, but not before she twisted her ankle and broke the heel off her boot. She cursed with every step until she was able to flag down a cab and return to her condo.

Seated in the wingback chair next to the window, Ann elevated her throbbing foot onto the ottoman and laid an ice bag on her swollen ankle. Already agitated that she had to throw away her ruined boots, she looked one last time at the page from the newsletter she held, the one Jane had mailed to her with the face of Karen circled, crumpled it into a ball, then threw it across the room.

Pensive, she glanced out of the window and watched the snowflakes drift to the ground. There was a time that the view of the park brought her solace. But now the bare, gray trees reminded her of the emptiness in her life—a life that a short time ago was filled with hope and promise of a future with family.

CHAPTER FORTY-EIGHT

They sat comfortably in bed, a tray of wine and cheese between them, and the original version of King Kong played on the movie channel. Michael looked at Meg who sniffled when the giant ape plummeted off the Empire State Building. Her sensitivity and compassion were extraordinary. He tenderly kissed her cheek and was amazed at the depth of his love for her.

She had her heart set on a fancy June wedding, but he would have been happy with a small private ceremony at City Hall. All he wanted was to make her happy so June it would be. He felt his passion grow, reached for her, and—

Ring. Ring.

Michael ignored the call, hugged her body close to his, kissed her softly, and—

Ring. Ring.

He groaned, kissed her shoulder, and said, "Don't go away." Michael turned over and grabbed the phone. "Vega."

"Hey buddy. It's Rizzo. I know it's late. Did I catch you at a bad time?"

"No, it's not a bad time." Michael mouthed the word 'sorry' to Meg. "I'm just watching a movie."

Meg gave him a thump on the arm, stuck her tongue out at him, and put the tv on pause.

"Vega, it's still circumstantial at this point, but you got my attention on this Paxton thing. I verified everything you said with a Sergeant Vernon down in Pinellas County, Florida, Preston's disappearance, and all the connections to the serial killer. Vernon told me she was a person of interest in the case.

"By the time deputies got there, her office and residence in Clearwater were empty, and both were wiped clean. They did find partial prints inside an open safe in her office. They ran the prints but didn't get a hit. The case went cold after they found her car submerged in Tampa Bay. Her body was never recovered."

"Uh huh." Michael said.

"Wait til you hear this . . . when Florida sent me Preston's driver's license and I compared it to Paxton's . . . unless they're twins or one of them is a doppelganger, I'm pretty sure it's the same person. I going to pay Ms. Paxton a little visit. I'll get back to you after I meet with her."

CHAPTER FORTY-NINE

The turning point in Ann's life was when she tricked the monster who molested Jane and her and shoved him down the stairs to his much-deserved death. From that day on, she had sacrificed her life to avenge those who could not protect themselves—Jane was the first and now she would be the last. The newspaper clippings that Ann kept in her 'kill file' since then, were a reminder of her life's mission. There were few incidents where she became emotionally involved. This was a vocation that required focus, determination, and precision planning. A lapse in judgement in any mission could lead to mistakes.

Now, she'd be going after the deceitful slut that shattered Jane's life and robbed Ann of a future with her sister.

Karen's pattern didn't change during the times Ann had followed her. It disgusted Ann to know Karen visit Gary's gravesite every morning before she went to work. She'd stand at the foot of his grave and sob. How dare she mourn Jane's husband. She bears the responsibility for his death, along with his wife.

Karen would join him soon enough, but Ann vowed that Karen would know agonizing pain first.

True to her fastidious nature, Ann eyed the contents of her organized closet, all of which was arranged by color and style. She removed her black woolen slacks and charcoal turtleneck sweater from the closet and dressed warmly for the night ahead. She then packed a careful selection of clothes; what clothes were left was bundled in trash bags and tossed into the trash shoot. She emptied the contents of the safe in her bedroom that included jewelry and the remaining money that she brought with her from Florida. Between the value of the jewelry and the cash, she had close to $600,000. It would be enough to start a new life with a new identity, alone.

There were hours before Karen finished her shift at the hospital which gave Ann sufficient time to complete her preparations. All evidence in her condo that could connect her to any of her missions was disposed of; the kill file, and the note and newsletter from Jane were shredded. She grabbed an empty mason jar from under the sink and placed it into her bag then meticulously as she did her office, she vacuumed, disposed of its contents, and wiped down every surface of her condo.

Her suitcase and tote were stuffed. Ann stood in the foyer taking in the sight of her condo. Convinced that she had addressed all that needed to be done, Ann checked that the pink stun gun and latex gloves were in her purse, then slung it over her shoulder. She closed the door and rolled behind her, the suitcase with the tote bag stacked on top. Ann shoved the bag of shredded documents into the trash shoot. Before she made it to the elevator, she heard her neighbor's door jerk open. Mrs. Bolinski called out to her.

"Are you going on a trip, Ms. Paxton?"

"No," Ann replied without regarding the woman.

"But I see you have suitcases."

"No, Mrs. Bolinski, I'm just taking my luggage for a walk!" Ann heard the busybody's door slam shut.

Aware of the numerous video cameras in the underground garage, Ann chose to put her luggage in the backseat rather than opening the trunk and exposing the bright red plastic gas container to a camera. To conceal the luggage from prying eyes, Ann draped the lap blanket she kept on the backseat, over the bags.

CHAPTER FIFTY

Parked at the pump of a mini mart a block away from where she had left the Malibu, the attendant filled the gasoline container that Ann brought with her. She paid with cash and thanked him politely as he secured the container in the back with a bungee cord, near the spare tire.

"Before you close the lid," Ann grabbed a couple of paper towels from the dispenser next to the pump and said, "would you mind wiping off that splash that's running down the side of the can?" and handed him the towels.

The young man huffed at her instruction then cautioned her about the risk of driving with gasoline in her car but said no more after Ann handed him a ten-dollar bill and assured him that she was only driving a short distance. She explained that her husband had run out of gas and was stranded on the side of the road and she was taking it to him.

Ann pulled away from the pumps and into an open space at the farthest corner of the lot. She locked the car and walked inside the minimart. On her return, she popped open the trunk and coughed at the heavy smell of gas, dry paper towels laid next to the plastic container. *Asshole didn't wipe it off.* There was nothing more for her to do at this point. The carpet was already damp.

She squeezed the contents of the charcoal lighter fluid she bought in the convenience store, into the mason jar from her kitchen, tightened the lid, and tossed the empty lighter fluid container onto the overflowing heap of trash that spilled out of the dumpster next to the building. She checked the emergency roadside kit that came with the car—everything was in order. She tucked the mason jar between the kit and the secured gas container.

She slid behind the steering wheel and removed from the bag the TracFone she also purchased while in the store. A piteous and disturbing scene nearby caught her attention. A young, heavily pregnant woman who couldn't be more than sixteen, was panhandling near the gas pumps. She took cash offered by a man in a pickup truck and hurried into the store. The girl came out with a bag in hand, sat on the retention wall next to the vacuum and air canisters, and devoured a donut and small carton of milk.

There was an aura around the pregnant young woman that demanded Ann's attention. Psychically, Ann knew she was in a situation that threatened her unborn child. Ann put the pre-paid phone down, picked up her purse, and got out of the car. She walked slowly toward the girl and asked, "May I join you?"

The girl seemed frightened and suspicious.

Not waiting for a reply, Ann lied and said, "I was once in your situation." Ann sat beside her and with a gentle demeanor, explained that she wanted to help and placed her arm around the wide-eyed girl's shoulders.

In a flood of emotion, the young woman broke down in tears and started to piece together her story of why she was forced to beg for money. She explained that she left a violent boyfriend who didn't want the baby and tried to kill it by beating her. Her family had disowned her when she got pregnant, and now she was desperate and had no place to go.

Ann opened her purse, wrote on the back of Mr. Bradley's business card, handed it to the girl, then tucked several hundred dollars into her hand. "First, get to a safe motel and get something nourishing to eat. Then, call that number and let Mr. Bradley know that Ann Paxton said you need the help of Scarlett's House Foundation now. I put the information on the back of his card."

No further discussion was necessary. Positive the expectant mother would do as instructed, Ann left the shocked girl sitting on the retention wall and returned to her car.

The TracFone was on the passenger seat. Ann used it to dial the hospital and waited for the operator to connect her to the emergency room desk. The call was answered by a man with a thick Spanish accent. Seconds passed before Ann understood the man to say that he'd page Nurse Chapman. It seemed forever before she answered.

"This is Nurse Chapman," she sounded annoyed. "May I help you?"

"My name is Ruth Greene," Ann faked a heavy Philadelphia accent, "I'm try'n to contact the nurse Karen Chapman that worked with Dr. Gary Mara. Am I speaking with the right Karen Chapman?"

There was a momentary silence before Karen replied, "What is this regarding?"

"It's a personal matter," Ann stayed in character. An awkward silence followed. Concerned that Karen might end the call, Ann continued as 'Ruth Greene.' "My husband and I own a jewelry store downtown. Dr. Mara was a good customer. He had a lovely piece engraved and said it was for years of dedicated service for his nurse, Karen Chapman."

Karen replied with a hint of skepticism, "Yes. I was Dr. Mara's nurse."

"Our store has been holding the item for him. Then I read about his unfortunate accident." Karen gasped. Ann continued, "It was a terrible shock. I'm so sorry. Since I didn't have your home information, I had to try to reach you at work. I don't normally make this type of call, but Dr. Mara was such nice man and a long-time customer, and he did pay for it in advance. It's quite expensive."

"Ms. Greene, thank you so much." Karen's tone was now devoid of suspicion. "Can you give me your address? My shift is over at seven tonight. I can stop by right after."

"Oh sweetie, our showroom is closing at five today for a month-long renovation. Not to worry though, I'll lock it in the safe until we re-open. You can pick it up then. At least we connected and now you know I'll be holding it for you."

"Oh, I'd hate to wait that long," Karen said. "Can you overnight it to me? I'll pay for the postage."

Slut, you're so predictable. "Sweetie don't worry. It'll be safe locked up in the store."

"Wait, wait. Let me see if I can get someone to cover for me. May I have your number and I'll call you right back."

"Um, hold on a minute, Ms. Chapman. Let me think . . . I have a better idea. I'm meeting my husband and some friends for dinner this evening at seven-thirty. I must go right past the hospital on my way, I'll be happy to drop it off to you. I'm sure you're anxious to get it."

The call ended with both women exchanging cellphone numbers and agreeing to meet in the main lobby of the hospital at seven.

Ann put the phone down on the console and took a deep breath. The energy of death surrounded her. Ann visualized with such intensity the blaze that would annihilate Karen, that she could almost feel the heat of the inferno. The whore would experience the fires of Hell before she died, the same agonizing death that Jane suffered.

Between the excitement of that image and the gasoline fumes emanating from the rear of her car, Ann experienced an odd exhilaration. Adrenaline coursed through her veins in anticipation of the night's events. She drove toward the isolated lot across the street from a vacant building—a dimly lit spot that was perfect to send Gary's lying mistress to join him. They could rot together through eternity. A proper karmic ending.

All that was left was to get her to this place.

CHAPTER FIFTY-ONE

Detective Rizzo from the Philadelphia Police Department stepped off the elevator and walked down the hallway to the office leased by Ann Paxton and saw that the door was open. He looked inside and discovered a man dressed in a khaki work uniform remove something from the desktop, wrapped it in paper towels, and placed it on his cart.

Rizzo tapped on the door. "I'm looking for Ann Paxton," he held up his badge. "I understand this is her office."

Startled, the man stood straight, and said, "I ain't stealin' nothin', sir."

"I'm not interested in what you might be putting in your cart. I'm trying to locate the woman who works here."

The man shrugged, and said, "I'm only the janitor, sir. All I know is I was told to clean her office. Not much to clean though. Looks like she was pretty neat."

"You don't have a problem if I take a look around, do you?"

"No sir. Help yourself."

Rizzo scanned the room for an indication of 'something.' He noticed a decorative cabinet across the room that appeared to be a safe. Its door was ajar. On further inspection, he saw the safe was empty. The detective asked the janitor, "If I peek in that cart of yours, am I going to find anything from this safe?"

"No sir, no sir. You can check it if you want. Only thing I got was an old clock off the desk and I ain't even sure if it works."

The detective took a final walk around the room. "What did you find in the trash can?"

"It was empty, sir. I thought it was brand new like nothin' was ever in it."

Rizzo looked at the name embroidered on the janitor's shirt. "Don't work too hard, Charlie. Have a nice day."

He stepped out of the Walnut Street building and into the bitter cold air. Rizzo walked down the block to a corner deli to grab something to eat. He sat at the counter and savored a bowl of hot soup while he jotted down some notes, finished his meal, and headed to Ann Paxton's apartment.

Detective Rizzo showed his badge to Hilmer, the concierge, and headed to the elevators. He stepped off on Ann Paxton's floor and walked directly to her apartment. He raised his hand to knock but turned at the sound of a click of a door lock.

Across the hall, a plump woman stepped out of her unit and wiped her hands on her apron. "I'm Mrs. Bolinski, can I help you?" she volunteered. "Are you here for Ms. Paxton? If you are, you just missed her. I think she was going on vacation."

"About how long ago did she leave?" Rizzo asked.

"Well, let's see, I had just started making my perogies, and my television show came on, so that was about four hours ago."

"Did she happen to mention where she was going?"

"I asked if she was going to Atlantic City, you know, she goes there a lot, but all she said was she was taking her luggage for a walk. Can you imagine? She was a bit testy. I try to be friendly, but she can be pretty sarcastic sometimes." The woman paused to take a breath. "Oh, um, are you a close friend of hers?" She stuttered, "Ah, uh, I didn't really mean sarcastic. If you give me your name, I can tell her you stopped by when she returns."

"That would be helpful." Detective Rizzo handed his business card to her.

The woman gasped at what she read. "Oh dear. You're a policeman . . . is everything alright?" anticipation on her face. "She's not in trouble, is she?"

"No ma'am. She's not in trouble. I just wanted to ask her a few questions." His posture was relaxed. "Do you know where she stays in Atlantic City?"

"I don't recall exactly where she stays, but I know it's at a very nice hotel. She IS pretty wealthy, you know. You have to be to live here. As a matter of fact, we have a couple of doctors and a senator who live on this floor." Mrs. Bolinski smiled with pride.

"Would you know if she's friends with anyone else who lives here?"

"Heavens no. I'm her only friend. As matter of fact, I was hurt that she didn't tell me where she was going—she usually does, and we were about to make plans to go shopping together."

"Mrs. Bolinski, you're obviously a good friend and neighbor, and well-informed. Would you let me know when she returns, or if you remember where she's staying in Atlantic City?"

"Oh my, well, of course I will. Yes, yes, I'll be happy to."

As the doors to the elevator closed, he could see Mrs. Bolinski who remained in the hallway. She waved and hollered, "I'll be in touch."

Before Rizzo left the building, he concluded a cursory interview of staff which revealed nothing remarkable about Ann Paxton. The consensus was that she was polite, kept to herself, and usually ate at the restaurant next door on Thursdays.

Detective Rizzo returned to the precinct, grabbed a can of root beer and his sandwich from the day before out of the breakroom refrigerator, and sat at his desk. He popped the top of the can, took a couple of gulps, and made a call to Michael Vega.

"Hi buddy, it's Rizzo. If you have a minute, I'd like to give you an update on Ann Paxton."

"Sure, go ahead," Michael replied.

"She's vacated her office on Walnut Street. I just left her apartment building. A neighbor saw her leave and said she thought she may be going to the shore.

I did speak with some of the staff in her building. This woman is so unremarkable that it's remarkable. I believe the best way to locate this Preston/Paxton character without alerting her is old fashioned leg work. We know what she drives, we know some of her habits, we're going to keep searching. I'll let you know when anything new turns up."

Michael was confident that Paxton was responsible for the attack on Trey Browning and that she would be arrested for that crime. From all that Connor said, Rizzo was a Pitbull. Once he latched onto something, he didn't let go. He would work this case to the end.

If there was any validity to what Allison claimed, Rizzo would also uncover the connections between Preston and Paxton and her involvement with the serial killer in Florida.

CHAPTER FIFTY-TWO

Ann timed her arrival in the working-class neighborhood to coincide with the least amount of outside activity, when the village idiots are home for dinner. She drove her Lexus to the side street where she had left the old Malibu getaway car and double-parked alongside. She checked her surroundings, and once assured it was safe, she quickly got out and transferred her possessions into the old clunker.

She drove away in the Lexus angered that she was forced to escape like a common criminal.

The impending event reinforced Ann's sense of power. Her heart began to pound with excitement. As cold as it was, she dabbed at the beads of perspiration on her upper lip. Filled with an incredible sense of righteousness, Ann made the call from the quiet of her car parked in the shadows of the secluded lot.

Karen answered the call on the second ring.

"Hi Karen, this is Ruth Greene."

"Oh, are you here already?" a note of elation in Karen's voice.

"No, Karen, and I do apologize. I'm not able to meet you tonight."

"Oh, no! I'm so disappointed."

"Sweetie, I'm disappointed too. I was on my way to you, but I got a flat tire and I'm sitting in a vacant lot waiting for AAA. The dispatcher said it may take an hour before they can get to me."

"That's not a problem." Karen offered, "I can wait for you."

"I'm really sorry, Karen, but it is a problem for me. My husband and friends will be at the restaurant waiting for me. I'll have to go directly there after they fix my tire. I'm so embarrassed. Perhaps I

213

made a mistake and got you all excited about this GORGEOUS gift for nothing. As I said before, I'll put it away and you can get it—"

"No, no, wait. Please, tell me where you are, and I'll be happy to come to you."

Ann rolled her eyes and smiled, then paused before she replied. "Well, I guess that would work, if you're sure it won't inconvenience you. I do have to wait here anyway."

She gave Karen her location.

Karen told her she knew exactly where the lot was. She'd passed it every day on her way home.

Ann mentally patted herself on the back for an outstanding performance as Ruth Greene. The greedy whore took the bait, hook, line, and sinker.

CHAPTER FIFTY-THREE

Except for a produce truck that went by, there was no traffic in the area. Ann checked the time on her phone, it was late. The whore should have been here already. *Did she catch on? She's not smart enough. Did she tell someone?* Blue and red strobing lights suddenly appeared and headed in her direction. Ann grabbed the steering wheel and reached for the starter. She let out a deep breath when the patrol car roared past her and made a sharp left turn onto a side street. Its lights disappeared into the darkness.

Within minutes, Karen's vehicle turned onto the lot, it's high beams lit the interior of Ann's car.

Ann flashed her headlights. Karen's SUV stopped next to her.

To keep Karen in her vehicle, Ann rushed to the driver side of the SUV and stood close enough to the door to prevent Karen from exiting. It forced Karen to lower her window.

"Hi. I'm Ruth. What perfect timing. The tow truck got here sooner than expected. They just left. You must have passed them."

"Ruth, thank you so much for waiting for me." Karen unlocked the doors and started to unbuckle her seat belt.

"Oh, Sweetie, don't get out. I'm already late but if I hurry, I can still make dinner on time. My husband will be so happy. The restaurant is holding the reservation." She reached inside her purse. "I have your very special gift right here." Ann handed Karen a small gift-wrapped box and reached again in her purse for the pink stun gun. While the whore was tearing into the paper, Ann zapped Karen on the side of her neck. The intensity of the voltage slammed her face-first on to the rim of the steering wheel. Ann knew she'd have no more than thirty seconds before Karen would come around.

Ann took from her purse, the zip ties she'd brought from home, wrenched open the door, grabbed Karen by the hair and yanked her back against the seat. A small cut had opened up over her eye. Ann reached for the right wrist of the unresponsive woman and tightly fastened it to the steering wheel. With seconds left before the effects of the stun gun wore off, Ann grabbed the woman's other hand and quickly zip tied it, as well.

To ensure her captive would stay immobilized, Ann pressed the stun gun to the woman and hit her again with full voltage. Karen's body jerked and twitched. Saliva drooled from the whore's mouth.

Ann retrieved the heavy container of gasoline from the trunk of her car and dumped part of the fuel on the ground under Karen's car inadvertently splashing the flammable liquid on her own shoes and pant cuffs. "Dammit!"

Without hesitation, Ann jerked open the rear door of the SUV, poured the remaining gasoline on the back seat, and tossed the can on the floor.

She returned to her car, removed the mason jar that she had filled with charcoal lighter fluid at the convenience store, and emptied it over the immobilized woman's head as if baptizing her for her entrance into Hell. The liquid ran down Karen's face and over the star ruby pendant that dangled from a gold chain around her neck.

The caustic fluid roused the dazed woman who coughed and gagged. Panic-stricken, Karen's fingers clawed into thin air. She groaned, "Why . . . are . . . you—" Again, she slumped against the steering wheel.

Ann threw the jar across the front seat. The jar hit the metal door handle.

She hurried back to the car, grabbed the flares from the emergency roadside kit, and struck the end cap across the top of one. It ignited immediately. A burst of brilliant light cut through the darkness that surrounded them.

"This is for Jane." Ann walked over to the window and tossed the lit flare into Karen's car, turned away immediately, struck the second flare and threw it in the trunk of her own car. She backed away rapidly and rushed across the dark street. Within seconds, the fumes from the fuel that seeped into the carpet caused the trunk of the Lexus to burst into flames. Ann increased her pace until she reached the sidewalk with little regard for possible voyeurs. She slowed and walked around the corner to the Malibu. Her thoughts were of all that Karen Chapman had taken from her.

There was a blast in the distance.

"Karma, Karen. Karma."

CHAPTER FIFTY-FOUR

Everything went according to plan. Ann was satisfied that Jane's death had been avenged in the appropriate karmic manner. A little breathless from the excitement of the event and her brisk walk, she sat behind the wheel of the old white car and listened to the wail of sirens. Front doors opened and residents poured out to see the commotion of fire engines that screamed past the end of the street. A surge of neighbors ran by her and toward the remote lot. There was another explosion. Two teenaged boys who rode on bicycles to the disturbance, whooped and hollered, "Aw, cool!"

How easily idiots are amused.

More sirens, more emergency vehicles.

Ann put the car into gear and pulled away from the curb, the Chevy's trunk filled with all of her earthly possessions she chose to take to start her new life in Arizona.

It took a great deal of time and effort to search on the internet, but she was able to find someone, for an exorbitant amount of money, who provided her with a new identity; social security number, driver's license, and all that she required. The existence of Ann Paxton ended tonight. It would be impossible for anyone to find her.

Another major challenge was to locate a realtor who would accept her three, five-thousand-dollar money orders to cover several months' rent in a temporary, but suitable area, with few questions asked, no background check required and the promise of a substantial cash bonus when Ann moved in.

This would be her first time in Sedona, but she was familiar with its reputation for beauty, unconventional personalities, and an abundance of energy vortexes. To ensure her privacy, Ann would explore the area alone and choose a residence in a secluded location. Once settled, she'd take her time to find the perfect place to open her office.

Ever the chameleon, Ann, would dress in southwestern Bohemian clothes to blend in with other metaphysical characters in the area. But, she doubted that she would ever get accustomed to wearing Birkenstocks. And of course, she'd have to change her hair . . . *maybe, black. It'll match my new name, Raven.*

A wet snow started to fall as she drove to Pittsburgh where she had made a reservation at a hotel not far from the Amtrak station. She'd grab a few hours of sleep first then find a side street somewhere in the area and dump the car with the keys in the ignition. Some half-witted hoodlum would surely take it.

Every detail of her 're-birth' as Raven Stephens had been covered, yet she couldn't relax completely until she and her belongings were inside the private room on the sleeper car she had reserved on the train for tomorrow's journey to Arizona.

Two hours into her drive, the heater in the car sputtered and stopped. Ann turned on the defroster. It blew nothing but cold air. "Piece of shit car!" She couldn't wait to get to the desert and out of this horrendous cold.

She thought about Jane and how she would have loved Sedona; the warm sun reflecting off the red soil, the blue sky.

WHOOSH! A tractor trailer weaved around her and splashed slush over her car.

"Asshole!" Ann turned up the speed on the wipers. All that did was smear icy mud over the windshield. The passenger side wiper stopped in mid swipe. "Oh great." She pushed the washer fluid button and nothing came out, but at least the wet snow helped to clear the windshield in front her.

Perturbed that the weather had slowed her down, she would arrive in Pittsburgh later than scheduled unless she could make up some time on the highway. At least when she stepped on the gas, there was more pick up than she expected. Before long she passed a road sign that read thirty-two miles to Pittsburgh. She was encouraged. She'd be there within the hour. The muscles in her neck and shoulders relaxed.

She peered in the side view mirror and saw in the distance, emergency lights fast approaching. The tractor trailer in front of her slowed down and moved into the right lane. She followed suit to allow the ambulance to pass.

As soon as the road was clear, Ann accelerated into the left lane and saw a cluster of red brake lights and a swarm of emergency vehicles up ahead.

"Aw shit!" The car in front of her had stopped dead. Ann slammed on the brakes. Her car spun out on the icy roadway. The glare of lights of the oncoming truck blinded her.

A piercing screech of brakes locking, and an air-horn blast were the last sounds she heard.

www.ingramcontent.com/pod-product-compliance
Lightning Source LLC
Chambersburg PA
CBHW061143170626
46809CB00003B/974

* 9 7 8 0 6 9 2 1 6 3 7 1 9 *